The Phantom of the Circus

The Phantom of the Circus

GILBERT MORRIS

Tyndale House Publishers, Inc.
Wheaton, Illinois

Library of Congress Cataloging-in-Publication Data

Morris, Gilbert.
    Barney Buck and the phantom of the circus / Gilbert Morris.
        p.   cm. — (The Ozark adventures ; 3)
    Summary: Fourteen-year-old Barney and his brothers try to find the
    person responsible for sabotaging the circus where the boys are working
    for the summer.
        ISBN 0-8423-5097-7
        [1. Circus—Fiction.   2. Christian life—Fiction.   3. Mystery and
    detective stories.]   I. Title.   II. Series: Morris, Gilbert.   Ozark
    adventures ; 3.
    PZ7.M8279Bas   1994
    [Fic]—dc20   94-9212

Printed in the United States of America

99   98   97   96   95
 7   6   5   4   3

TO ALLAN
"A wise son maketh a glad father."

Contents

1

Jake's Plan

OH, Barney, just think. We don't have to go to school again for three whole months!"

Debra Simmons threw her arms around me and just about squeezed me to pieces! She was one of the smartest and prettiest girls in Cedarville for her age—which was fourteen, the same as mine—but she hadn't caught on to how to behave, you know?

About ten million times I'd explained to her we were just *pals*. Well, in a way it worked out like that. Debra liked to hunt and fish and knew *almost* as much about trailing a bluetick hound as I did. She wasn't silly and always giggling like a lot of her girlfriends.

But smart as she was, she just couldn't seem to realize

that, no matter how much she ran dogs on the coon trail with me in the woods, she was also a *girl*.

That was why when she grabbed me and hugged me, I squirmed away. "Hey, Debra," I said, "you wanna be careful about hugging me! Somebody might get the wrong idea."

"What idea?" she demanded.

"You know what I mean, Debra. I've explained it to you a thousand times. We're just good friends, like we've agreed."

"We have?" she murmured in that deep voice of hers, then gave me one of those long glances that turned my knees to mush and made me stutter.

"Now stop that, Debra!" I said, clearing my throat. "Come on, let's make some supper."

Her grandpa—Uncle Dave Simmons to us—was skinning some coons. So Debra and I puttered around the kitchen getting some bacon and eggs and biscuits ready. I put some refrigerator dough into a pan, turned on the oven, and shoved the pan into it. Debra got the eggs and bacon out of the refrigerator. While she was frying the bacon, she kept talking about how nice it would be to have the whole summer off with no books. Ordinarily I would have agreed with her, but something was bothering me.

While we were waiting for the biscuits to get brown, I finally interrupted her. "Sure I'm glad school's out, but

I won't be loafing much. We've all got to work and try to save a little money."

We meant me and my two brothers. Jake was twelve, and Joe was ten. When our parents had died in an auto accident about two years ago, we'd come to live on our dad's old home place in Goober Holler. The Chicago judge who dealt with orphans and foster kids agreed to our coming only because Miss Jean stood up for us. She was a juvenile officer there and was going to marry Coach Dale Littlejohn, who taught in the school where we went. They were going to adopt the three of us, and we would all live right here.

That would've been *great,* but Miss Jean decided to get her master's degree at a university before she and Coach got married. Now my brothers and I had to live on the money from a trust fund our dad left for us. It wasn't a lot of money. That was why we had to work all we could to make it last. During summers, we had to find jobs to help us buy clothes and stuff for the next school year.

I explained all this to Debra, and by the time I was finished, the biscuits were done. "I'll go get Uncle Dave while you pop those eggs in the skillet," I said. "I want mine over easy. Don't let them get too hard."

"After some of the stuff *you've* cooked, Barney, anything I do will be an improvement!"

That's exactly right, I thought as I opened the door

and called Uncle Dave. "Hey! Supper's ready! Come and get it."

"Right with you, boy!" Uncle Dave was already through with the coons. I could see by the bare light bulb we'd strung up behind the house that he'd already skinned them and put them on a rack. "I'm hungry as a bear!"

Uncle Dave Simmons was eighty, but he could out-walk just about any of the young men in Clark County. He was tall as a pine tree and just as straight. He had sharp black eyes and skin that looked like leather. He'd also taught me all I knew about coon dogs and hunting.

"Let's eat!" he said, and the three of us sat down just as the eggs were ready. After Uncle Dave asked the blessing, we sank our teeth into the crisp bacon and those soft fried eggs, done just right. The biscuits were golden brown and so soft and flaky they melted in my mouth. We had mild sorghum molasses over our biscuits and plenty of hot coffee (for Uncle Dave, of course!) and fresh milk to wash them down with.

Finally Uncle Dave pushed his plate away. "Boy, that was *prime!* After running a bluetick hound for about a hundred miles after a boar coon, vittles like that go down right good!" He grinned at me and added, "For a city boy, you've done right good."

I got a little red like I always did when somebody said something nice about me. A dumb scar on my forehead, where my brother Jake clipped me once, always stood up like a flag—along with my dumb freckles—when I blushed. Add red hair and a frame like a stork, and you've got what I looked like.

Debra saw I was tongue-tied, so she said, "Granddad, Barney needs a job for the summer. If you hear of anything, tell him about it."

"Well, I guess maybe something will turn. . . ." He stopped, then said, "Car's coming." He had ears like a red fox, and a few seconds later I heard it, too.

"That's probably Coach bringing Jake and Joe home from the circus," I commented.

"Oh? Is the circus in town?" Uncle Dave asked.

We'd been in the woods running coons every night and sleeping days, so I hadn't gone. "They were dying to go, and Coach promised to take them tonight," I said.

Brakes squealed. It was just like Coach to slam them. He drove a fancy Camaro like a racing car driver. Miss Jean said he'd stop soon enough when *she* got married to him. He would then grin, which would turn her to Silly Putty! Coach Littlejohn was almost the spitting image of Robert Redford, only better looking. He'd been an all-American cornerback at Alabama, and I guess if he'd told me to jump off the peak at Panther Gap, I would've done it.

Now he came in looking like something out of *Gentleman's Quarterly*—all decked out in gray flannel slacks and a fawn-colored suede sports coat. But he sure didn't look like a wuss! He had a wedge-shaped face with white teeth that gleamed and dark eyes that had melted most of the girls in Clark County—before he'd met Miss Jean, of course!

"Hey, how about some of that grub?" Coach grinned, plopping down onto a chair. Debra got up right away and started waiting on him. I wished I could've had the kind of power he had!

Jake and Joe came in and asked for some food, too. Jake was short, wide, and took after our great-grandma Buck, a Native American (which he partly is). He was also a throwback to one of our ancestors who must have been a real operator. Jake was always coming up with some wacky scheme to get rich quick, and those dumb ideas of his usually got *me* into hot water!

Joe was fair-skinned, with mild blue eyes like our mom's. He couldn't read or write too well because he had dyslexia, which I couldn't understand. It didn't bother Joe. He was an inventor—always making things you never heard of. One of the teachers at school had said that Joe was a genius! Joe didn't have to read, because he could *synthesize*—meaning he could take all kinds of ideas and invent machines to do just about *anything!*

He'd invented a catapult to shoot people off into the Caddo River, as well as all kinds of stuff around the house. The coffeepot came on by itself and had coffee ready when we got up, and Joe was working on a computer of some kind that did weird things.

Debra kept dishing out the bacon and eggs and biscuits until everyone was stuffed. Then Jake looked right at me and announced with a grin, "Barney, our troubles are over!"

I stared at him. "Wait a minute, Jake. Don't tell me you've found a way to make us rich, healthy, and good-looking!"

He grinned, picked up a biscuit, and stuffed it into his mouth. "Well, I can't guarantee the *good-looking* part—especially with *you*. . . ." He gave Uncle Dave a broad wink, then swallowed the biscuit. Jake never *chewed* anything! "But I've got a plan lined up that will make us rich!"

"You're not going to get us into raising minks again, are you?" I asked. "Or fishing worms? And I hope we don't have to sell those fire extinguishers that blew up and ruined Johnson's Hardware Store." These had all been Jake's little schemes. They had cost us a fortune and nearly got us put into jail.

Jake turned and glared at me like Geronimo in a bad mood. "Well, shoot, Barney. I can't *always* be right! But *this* time, it's a surefire thing!"

"What is it Jake?" Uncle Dave asked with a wide grin. "Gonna invest in wildcat oil stocks?"

"All right, all *right,*" Jake grumbled, his black eyes

glaring. He waited until we'd stopped laughing before he said, "This is a sound business proposition, and we'd be *crazy* not to take it."

"All right, Jake, what is it?" I asked.

"Why, we're gonna be in the circus this summer!" he said with a wide grin. "And by the time school starts, we'll have so much money we can all wear shirts with alligators on them—like Coach!"

Coach turned a little red—he always did when we teased him about his fancy clothes. "Never mind my alligators! I want to go on record as saying I think the whole idea is downright *dumb!*"

Usually that would've been enough. I had so much confidence in Coach Littlejohn that whatever he said was *it!*

But my brother Jake held some sort of strange power over me. Even now I can't explain it. Whenever he started in on me with one of his fruitcake ideas— even though I knew it would probably put scars on my fair, white body—before long he'd have me into it body and soul.

"Well, let's have it," I groaned and threw myself back into my chair with my hand over my heart. "I suppose I'll be the one to stick my head in the lion's mouth— since I'm the oldest!" Jake always threw something like that at me whenever there was an unpleasant or dangerous job to be done.

8

He looked hurt. "I'm surprised at you, Barney! After all I've done to see that we make a lot of money . . ."

"And have a swell time, too!" Joe ran around the table and pulled at my arm, babbling like a brook. "We get to feed the animals and help put up the tent, and we get to go all over with the circus, Barney! Let's do it, huh? Please, Barney?"

Well, if I had trouble saying no to Jake, it was ten times worse with Joe! He was such a good kid, and he looked so much like our mom that it was just impossible for me to deny him anything. He never wanted anything for himself.

"Look, it's real simple, Barney," Jake said in that grown-up bargaining voice of his. "I went around after the show last night and got to meet Mr. Cortina—he owns the circus, but he's one of the performers, too. Well, I told him we were looking for summer jobs, and he said we could work all summer for the circus. Isn't it great?"

"Yeah, I guess it is." Actually, I got quite a thrill out of the idea myself. I'd been to only a couple of circuses in Chicago, but they had always been so good I thought about them for weeks! And now the thought of being a part of anything that was so much fun made me kind of dizzy.

"Barney!" Coach said, with a little frown. "It may sound exciting, but Jake's not telling *all* of it. The truth is that this circus is on its last leg—almost ready to fold. *That's* why Cortina was so ready to offer jobs to three untrained kids."

"It does sound funny," Debra said. "How could they pay you if they're broke?"

"On *shares!*" Jake shouted. "All right, so they're in a bind." Jake looked more like Geronimo than ever. "Every business has a few problems. But here's what they've done. All the circus people—performers and all the rest—have agreed to work for no salary, but for a share of the profits. And that's what we'd get, see?"

"And what if there *are* no profits?" Coach demanded.

"There will be!" Jake said stubbornly. "Mr. Cortina has it all figured out that if nothing bad happens, all the debts will be paid and all the performers will make a big profit."

"Sounds like a risky business," Uncle Dave said, drumming his fingers on the table. "Better think twice about it, Barney."

"It would be dumb!" Debra added. "You'd be gone all summer."

Well, we all talked about it for most of the evening. When the visitors had gone home and the three of us had gone to bed, I somehow felt that no matter how crazy it was, the Bucks of Goober Holler would be under the big top after all!

2
Meeting an Angel

STEP right up! Hurry! Hurry! Hurry! The show won't start for twenty minutes!"

A skinny man in a bright plaid suit barked loudly as we walked by his wooden platform with its big canvas sign fluttering in the breeze. We had all come—Uncle Dave, Debra, Coach—and, of course, Jake and Joe for the fourth time.

Joe pulled me to a stop. "Look at that, Barney!" he said. "The strongest man in the world, right here in Cedarville!"

Right beside the skinny man was a huge man with hair white as cotton and baby blue eyes. He was taking his robe off, and we could see he was knotted all over with muscles. He bent over and picked up a big barbell as if it were made of air, his muscles rippling like snakes.

We stopped and listened as the skinny man told us all about the Living Skeleton, the Fattest Woman in the World, the Plastic Man, and a lot of other "unusual people," as he called them.

"Let's don't go in," Debra said, "I don't like things like that."

"Why, they're just people, Debra," Joe said with a smile. "We went to the trailer with some of them last night. Mr. Spence—the Living Skeleton—was born not too far from where we lived in Chicago, and he was in the same part of the army as our dad during the war."

Debra walked away, and we all followed her.

The Cortina Brothers' Circus was set up on the county fairgrounds. The big top was over at the end toward the Little League ballpark, and you had to go on a type of lane to get to it. On one side stood a lot of booths where you could win stuffed animals by tossing a ring over a stick, but not very many people seemed to win. There were all kinds of places to buy cotton candy, hot dogs, candied apples, cider, and Cracker Jack. On the other side, two long, skinny tents stretched along the way. One of them was the freak show—what they called "unusual people." Right past it was the menagerie.

"We can buy our tickets there," Jake said importantly. "Your treat, I think you said, Uncle Dave?"

"That's what *you* said I agreed to, Jake." Uncle Dave cocked his head and gave Jake a hard look. "I knew you'd figure out some way to get in for nothing—and I guess I'm it."

He stopped and bought tickets for all of us, and we went into the long tent, Jake leading the way and pointing out the animals as if they were his. "Those are the lions that Rex Rogers uses in his act," he said, pointing at a cage full of large, nervous cats. "And those are the leopards, and there's the most fierce tiger on the North American continent!"

"You been practicing up to be a barker, Jake?" Coach asked with a grin.

"Well, he *is!*" Jake said with a stubborn nod. "And just wait until Rex gets into that cage with all of those cats at the same time. *Then* I guess you'll see!"

"It stinks in here!" Debra said, wrinkling up her nose and pulling at my arm. "Let's go. Who wants to see a lot of animals all caged up?"

Jake protested, but I was ready. I'd never liked zoos or any place where they penned animals up. I'd even felt sorry for the ponies they kept outside the Wal-Mart stores for little kids. Once I had a plan to steal the ponies and take them someplace where they could walk on soft green grass instead of on that hot concrete. But the ponies would've been replaced.

We went on inside anyway. I'd seen only two circuses,

but they were both big ones. They'd been inside large arenas and had had three rings with entertainment going on in all three of them at once.

The Cortina Brothers' Circus had two small rings and one large ring in the center. Something was going on most of the time in the two small rings—a clown or two fooling around, or maybe just a single person doing a tumbling act. All the big acts took place in the large center ring.

"Not very big, is it?" I said when we'd gotten seated. We had a good spot right in front of the center ring.

"Mr. Cortina says nobody can watch three rings at the same time," Joe said. "He says in Europe, where the really *good* circuses are, they nearly all have just one ring."

"That makes sense to me," Uncle Dave said with a nod. "Never could see any sense in takin' people's attention off the big show with a lot of fritterin' around!"

"Here comes the grand parade!" Joe shouted as a brassy circus band near our left broke out into a loud march. We all turned to watch, and a man on a horse shot out of the entrance and raced around the track. He got just about even with us, then threw up his hands and seemed to push himself off backwards! I thought he was gone for sure! Debra screamed, and Uncle Dave gave a grunt. Then the rider caught himself by one heel, swung over the hooves of the horse, went underneath the animal, then was up again, neat as you please!

"Say, that fellow isn't bad!" Coach said with a whistle.

"Bad?" Uncle Dave snapped. "Not *bad?* Sonny, that feller is so good he made me swallow my chewin' tobacco!"

Well, it wasn't a big parade, but it was sharp, you know? The clowns were active, tumbling all over the place and throwing water (really just paper) at the crowd. The acrobats looked as sleek as seals in their gleaming white tights, and the elephants scared a lot of kids by reaching over with their rubbery trunks to beg for peanuts.

Then the parade was over. All the lights went out except for a spot in the exact center of the big ring. A tall, heavy man with a big handlebar mustache was standing there in a bright red suit with black boots and a tall black hat. He took off his hat and said in a voice you could have heard in Chicago, "Ladeeeeeez and gentlemen! Welcome to 'The Greatest Show on Earth'—The Cortina Brothers' Circus!" The band blared and everybody cheered a little. He went on, "And right now, direct from triumphant tours of Europe and Asia, in the center ring, I give you Rowena and her white stallions!"

A beautiful woman wearing shorts, a long frock-tailed coat, and a high hat came prancing out of the dark, leading five of the prettiest milk-white horses I've ever seen. She could make them do almost anything.

"Oh, isn't she beautiful!" Debra said.

I glanced at her sparkling eyes. "Well, she's pretty, but look at those *horses!*"

Debra gave me a look that would have soured milk and then sniffed as she turned back to watch the act. "You have no romance in your soul, Barney Buck!" she snapped.

But I did.

It really got to me, that circus! I was sitting so close I could see the rubber band that held on the clown's big ball of a nose. I could see the strain in the face of the bottom acrobat holding up six people, how the sweat ran down his face and got into his eyes. But he didn't dare do more than blink, or his fellow performers would fall with a crash. I could see the funny red tongue of Rajah, the Bengal tiger, as he roared and swiped at Rex Rogers with claws sharp as swords!

I saw mistakes, too. Sometimes the acrobats were off balance and fell to one knee, and the third white horse of Rowena stumbled and threw the other horses out of step. Once the tiny young woman on the high wire slipped. Her eyes grew wide as she tried with all her strength to catch her balance—and nobody in the tent breathed until she did. Then we all jumped up and gave her a standing ovation.

It was *real* is what I'm trying to say. I could tell they didn't have enough help. Some of the acrobats had to move their own equipment around, and even though they tried hard, it was obvious that the Cortina Brothers' Circus was having problems.

Then came the last act—the Flying Cortinas. "Watch this!" Jake whispered importantly with a wave of his hand. "You haven't seen *anything* yet!"

The spotlight followed two men and two women as they came out from the side wing. They were wearing pure white capes covered with sequins, which glittered like diamonds under the blue lights. They all had the same dark hair and olive skin, but the younger man looked different.

"I present to you . . . ," the ringmaster boomed, "Thomas Cortina, the world's greatest catcher; his wife, Lillian Cortina; and their daughter Angel, who at the ripe old age of fourteen is one of the most accomplished fliers in the world! And Juan del Rio, the youngest man in the world ever to accomplish a triple somersault!"

The four walked to the center ring to the beat of the music, then removed their capes and went to the top of the big tent. Thomas Cortina took the large rope in his big hands and began lifting himself hand over hand, his upper body rigid and his legs bent and pointing like a ballet dancer's at a sharp angle. He went up so smoothly you'd think he had been made of feathers!

His wife did the same. Juan did it next even easier. Finally the girl named Angel took the rope and seemed to float up it.

"That's quite a trick right there," Coach said.

"That girl," I said with a grin, "makes most *boys* look sick—the way she went up that rope!"

Debra gave me a look. "I might've *known* you'd be watching *her!*"

I opened my mouth to protest my innocence, but Uncle Dave gave me a poke in the ribs with his elbow and whispered in my ear, "Keep shut, boy! It's the only way to reason with a female!"

The Flying Cortinas were really something. The circus had some good acts and some not so good, but these people were in a class by themselves. I mentioned this to Coach, and he nodded. "You're right. They're world-class acrobats, Barney. And they didn't get that way in a month. They've been practicing all their lives to do that!"

By "that" he meant the sudden somersault that Juan del Rio did in midair. It looked easy, but as I watched him clamp his hands onto Thomas Cortina's wrists, I knew they'd spent long hours of hard work practicing these acts.

Lillian Cortina was good, and Angel was even better. But it was Juan del Rio who did all the really hard stuff. He didn't do the triple, but he did a double. I just about bit my tongue off when he flew off that bar, went into a ball, and came out of it like a cannonball, meeting Thomas Cortina's hands so hard both of them rocked on the bar!

My hands were sore from clapping, and my throat was raw when the act was over, but I wasn't alone. The audience kept on clapping while the Flying Cortinas took one bow after another until they finally slipped away and the lights came up so we could leave the tent.

"Come on," Jake said as we got out of the Big Top. "We've got an appointment. With Mr. Cortina."

He led us all through the small openings between the Big Top and the menagerie tent to a group of trailers and motor homes lit by a few naked bulbs. "Don't fall over the guy lines," he said. "There's the trailer right there."

"We can't just go busting in like this," I protested.

"Sure we can. Mr. Cortina said to bring you in right after the show." Jake marched right up to the door of the largest trailer and knocked with authority. He did everything with authority.

The door opened, and a shaft of yellow light shot out. Outlined in the door was Thomas Cortina. He smiled and stepped back. "Ah, my friend Jake and his friends. Come in. Please come in."

Jake went in first, then the rest of us. It was a roomy trailer, but we filled it up pretty well. Besides Mr.

Cortina, there were his wife, Lillian, and his daughter, Angel. Jake introduced us, and then Mr. Cortina said, "Sit down, please. You will excuse us for not being prepared for guests. We have been busy lately."

We all found a place to sit, and I noticed the place was clean with nice furniture. Then my eyes met Angel's, and she gave me a smile that wiped me out. All I could do was look down and pick at my sleeve!

"I hope you enjoyed the show," Mr. Cortina said. We all nodded and said how much we liked it. "I suppose Jake has told you of my offer—jobs for all three of you boys for the summer?"

"Mr. Cortina, I'm responsible for the boys—not legally as yet—but I'll be adopting them as soon as possible," Coach said. I was glad he was there. He looked like nobody to fool with, and when he talked, people listened.

"Oh, you are married?" Lillian Cortina smiled.

That made Coach blow his cool. "Well, I *practically* am . . . and . . . well, anyway, I'll have to insist on a few bits of information if I'm to let the boys go with the circus."

"Ahhhh," Mr. Cortina said with a smile. He leaned back and shook his head at Coach. "You have heard about what *wicked* people we show business people are, Mr. Littlejohn! Is that not so?" He laughed and shook his head. "No, no, that is quite all right. I am happy that the Buck brothers have a friend who will take such an interest in them. But you may rest easy. We may seem quite exotic to you, but actually we are a very ordinary family. I will be happy to give you references from some people who will vouch for us—my banker, the attorney general of my home state, my pastor. . . ."

That caught Coach's attention. "Your pastor? You're Christian people?"

Mr. Cortina gave his wife a smile. "Oh yes. You also?"

"Sure he is," Jake piped up. "He's a Sunday school teacher and a deacon!"

"Fine, fine!" Mr. Cortina smiled. "You have my word that the boys will be in church every Sunday, Mr. Littlejohn. Along with the rest of us, right, Angel?"

"I'll be glad to take them with me," Angel said with a smile. I heard Debra mumble something, but I couldn't make it out. Then Angel said, "Why don't I take Barney out and show him the rigging, Daddy? Isn't that what he'll be working on—if he decides to come?"

"Yes, you do that, Angel. Lillian, you might show Joe and Jake here what they'll be doing if they decide to come with us."

Angel got up and headed for the door. "Come on, Barney. I'll show you the world of the Flying Cortinas."

I heard Mr. Cortina talking to Coach and Uncle Dave about our jobs. Then I stumbled across the ground, trying not to fall over one of the ropes that kept the Big Top upright.

"How old are you, Barney?" Angel asked.

"Going on fifteen," I said, then wondered why I hadn't said "fourteen," like I usually did.

"So am I," she said.

"Oh, I thought you were older." The ringmaster had said she was fourteen, but I'd thought it was show business talk. Actually I thought she was fifteen or even sixteen. I looked down at her and noticed that she looked a lot younger up close than she did far off.

"My, you *are* nice and tall, Barney!" she said with a smile. As usual, whenever a pretty girl paid any attention to me, it ruined my speech habits. I always blushed and talked gibberish that even *I* couldn't understand! In situations like this, I would usually try not to say any more than I had to.

Angel didn't wait for me to make a fool out of myself. We walked over to the tent, and she showed me how the equipment worked. Of course, I didn't understand a tenth of it. Finally she sat down on the rim of the center ring and patted the spot beside her. "Sit down, Barney, and tell me about yourself."

Well, I got myself together and, by not looking right at her, I was able to tell about how we'd lost our parents and were mostly waiting for Coach and Miss Jean to get married so we could have a real home.

She listened, and when I finished, she said softly, "I'm so glad you're going to have a real home soon, Barney." Then she blinked a few times, and I noticed she was about to cry.

"Hey! Please don't cry about me!"

"Oh, I'm not, Barney—not about *you*. It's . . . it's just that it looks like I'll lose my home pretty soon."

"Your home?"

"The circus." She waved her hand around the arena, empty and silent now. "Didn't Jake tell you about how we have only this one summer to make enough to save the show?"

"Well, he did mention something about it, but I didn't know it was so serious."

"It is to us—to my father. He's worked all his life to have his own circus. Now—if a miracle doesn't happen, he's . . . he's . . ."

Angel leaned right against me, and with my being so tall, she just sort of fit right against my chest, and I couldn't help but put my arms around her. Then I gave her a little pat and muttered, "Aw, don't worry. It'll be all right!"

Finally, after she'd sobbed and sobbed, she pulled back and smiled up at me. "Thank you for not laughing at me, Barney. You're a very fine boy. I can see that!"

"You *ought* to be able to see it. You're certainly *close* enough!"

It was Debra. She'd come up right behind us. I don't guess she'd actually snuck up on us, but when she spoke up, I jumped off that ring like it was turned to white-hot steel.

"Why . . . uh . . . hello, Debra." Boy, I sure had some way with words.

"Why . . . uh, hello, Barney," she shot right back. I always thought it was cute the way Debra could mimic just about anybody. It didn't seem so cute right then!

"We're leaving," she said, staring at Angel but talking to me. "Do you want to come, or are you planning to stay here permanently?"

"Oh, sure, I'm ready," I said.

Debra then said with a smile that somehow wasn't a smile, "Good night, Miss Cortina. I certainly enjoyed your *act!*"

"I'm sure you did," Angel said. "I'll try to do as well in the future."

"I believe *that!*" Debra said, walking away from her. I had to run to keep up with her as we made our way back to the car, where the others were waiting.

I got in, and all the way home everybody was talking at once—mostly about whether or not we should take the job.

Uncle Dave argued that we shouldn't. "I think they'll go bust, and then you wouldn't get a cent."

"I guess you're probably right, Uncle Dave," Coach said. "They're good people, though. I wouldn't mind trusting the boys to them as far as that goes."

24

And, of course, Jake and Joe were practically down on their knees begging to go. Jake even promised to *behave*—something he'd never done before!

Finally I decided that no matter how much fun it might be, we just couldn't take the gamble. We needed money too much for the next year. I was just about to speak up and say so when Debra piped up in a cold, hard voice that didn't sound at all like her.

"Barney is not going to waste his summer at that nasty ol' circus!"

As soon as she'd said *that,* I got mad! I glared at her and said in my toughest voice, "We're not going to miss a chance like this because *someone* doesn't want us to do it!"

It was as quiet as a tomb the rest of the way home. When Coach let Debra and Uncle Dave out, I was just about ready to admit I was wrong. Then Debra turned and snapped, "I hope you get swallowed by that mangy old lion, Barney Buck!"

I got mad all over again. Then Jake put the icing on the cake. He leaned out and hollered loud enough to break glass: "Don't worry, Debra. Barney won't get eaten. He'll have Angel to watch over him, won't he?"

I think Debra threw a rock at him—or was it at me? It hit the back of Coach's Camaro with a *ping,* and I knew that somehow Jake had won again. We would be working for the circus!

3
First-of-May

HEY, First-of-May! Tell the butcher in the backyard to stay away from the bulls. We have some cherry pie for him before doors."

That was shouted at me by a clown with a huge grin painted on his face and pink hair in fuzzy masses all over his head, and a red rubber ball for a nose. The clown then gave me a shove. He must have noticed I was shaken up, because he stopped and came up to where I was standing beside the tiger cage. Over the blare of the circus band, he said, "You must be the new rigger I heard about."

I just stared at him. "I'm Felipe Cortina," he continued, "brother of Thomas. Call me Felipe." He pronounced it

Fay-leep-ay. He had warm brown eyes set off in the white-and-red paint on his clown face. "Look, kid, a *First-of-May* is just somebody new to the circus work, because that's when they started in the old days, see? A *butcher?* Anybody who sells hot dogs and sodas. The *backyard* is here, just by the entrance, and a *bull* is any elephant—even if it's a lady elephant!" He grinned at me, and I felt a little better.

"What's *cherry pie*—and *doors?*" I asked.

"*Cherry pie* is extra work, and *doors* means that the crowd is comin' in to take their seats." Then he picked up his head as the band broke into a loud march. "There's the Grand Parade. Pass the word, will you kid?" Then he shot out of the menagerie tent and headed toward the Big Top. I just stood there feeling helpless.

Just twenty-four hours before, I had decided to join the circus, and I hadn't slept a wink since!

Once we'd made up our minds, we needed to get some things done. I had to see that Tim, my black-and-tan hound, would be cared for by Chief Tanner. Jake's fancy Chinese chickens (which were going to make us all rich!) had to be boarded at Sonny Tatum's place. Joe had to get Ronnie Millington to agree to feed his prize-winning heifer, Agnes. We had to tend to ten million other little details. Finally we just sort of gave up. We locked the house, gave Uncle Dave the key, and just hoped for the best.

I'd tried to see Debra, but she'd been hiding out from me; so we'd piled into Uncle Dave's Jeep, and he'd dumped us off with our suitcases at the Cortina Brothers' Circus just an hour before the last performance at Cedarville started.

Angel had spotted us and had come running up. She was already wearing her special snow-white tights and cape, but she caught me by the arm, her eyes sparkling. "You'll stay with my Uncle Felipe, Barney. Come and I'll show you!" She called out to the cotton-haired strongman, "Heck, this is Jake and Joe. Show them your trailer, will you please?"

She pulled me quickly to the trailer park and opened the door to a pale green fifth-wheel trailer hitched to a four-wheel drive Ford 150. "I've already talked to my Uncle Felipe. He says you'll have this room all to yourself. It's very nice, isn't it?"

She pulled me inside and showed me a little bedroom in the front section of the trailer—the part that mounted to the truck. It was as clean as a pin, and there were windows looking out on three sides of a full-sized bed with a blue spread. "Put your clothes in that chest, and there's the bath. But come now and I'll show you what you must do tonight."

She dragged me back to the Big Top and again went over the different wires and ropes that the Flying Cortinas used in their act. This time I managed to make sense of about half of it. She ended hurriedly, "Tonight we'll pack, and then you'll learn how to take the rigging down. Now I must go."

It was like getting caught in some sort of busy factory where everybody knew what he was doing—except *me!* Clowns were helping with the equipment, riggers were pulling wires and tying off ropes, people were moving the animals from one cage into a chute—and I was just standing there like a ninny!

That was when Felipe the clown had found me, and I'd managed to pass the word on. Then I saw Thomas Cortina talking to the ringmaster and waving his hands like a windmill. Both of them were shouting. I edged closer, and when Mr. Cortina had finished, he saw me.

"Ah, Barney!" He smiled and came and put his hand on my shoulder. "I am happy you and your brothers will be with us! Now, it will be very confusing at first, but you will learn. Just stay close to me and do what you are told. Soon you will be an expert rigger. I guarantee it!"

Well, mostly I just kept myself from getting stepped on by the bulls—the elephants—and from doing any damage as the show went on. I kept my eyes open, and by the time it was over, I had a pretty good idea of how to handle the *webs*—the long ropes that hang down from the top of the arena. All of the aerialists did their tricks on them, and I found out that the men who stand on the ground holding the bottom of the ropes were called *web-sitters*.

Finally the Flying Cortinas did their act, and the band played the last piece. After the audience filed out, I thought I'd have a chance to rest up a little. Was I ever wrong!

"You Barney?" a midget in a clown costume asked abruptly. "I'll show you how to break down the rigging."

"Right *now?*" I asked.

He stared at me, then laughed. "You *are* First-of-May!" he bellowed in a bullfrog voice. "We gotta be packed and on our way by three o'clock. You watch me—'cause you'll be doin' this job when we leave our next stop. C'mon, Barney. You're a razorback now!"

"A *razorback?*" I asked, trotting to keep up with him. "What's that?"

"Guys that tear down a circus and put it up again." The midget got to the center ring and, to my amazement, scampered like a monkey up the rope that led to the trapeze! "Well, you want a special invitation?" he shouted at me.

I did the best I could to climb the rope ladder that led to the high perch in the center ring. I'd never been at my best in high places. Then the midget hollered down, "Oh, by the way, my name's Lou Beauchamp." He pronounced it *Beech-um*. He started taking the wires and ropes down and naming them all, and I had to hang on with one hand and catch the falling ropes with the other!

The whole Big Top was a beehive. Everywhere I looked, people were shouting and things were being yanked apart. It was like a bomb going off in slow motion. The rings were being demolished, the ropes untied and dangling loosely, the canvas was swaying dangerously. I had the feeling that everything was caving in on me!

Somehow it all got done. The tent came down with help from the bulls as they allowed the big tent poles to drop gently to the earth. The equipment was dismantled and packed into huge trucks waiting with open doors—like hippos with their mouths open to swallow the loads of canvas, wood, steel, and human cargo.

Then I heard the trucks cough like huge beasts with a roar that shook the ground, their lights shooting out into the darkness. The Cortina Brothers' Circus slowly uncoiled like a snake and seemed ready to leave Cedarville behind.

A small, wiry man with a dark face pulled at me and shouted, "Well, you going with the circus, Barney? Or you going to take root here?"

I gaped at him, finally recognizing Felipe Cortina without his clown makeup. He led me to the cab of his truck, then ignored me as he found his place in the caravan of trailers and cargo trucks that threaded its way out of town and turned onto Interstate 40, heading south. "We gotta be in Biloxi and set up by tomorrow night," was all he said.

"But that's over four hundred miles away!" I said.

He gave me a tired grin. "Way it goes, Barney."

Well, I'd missed one night's sleep, but I caught a few winks with my head bumping against the window of Felipe's pickup. I was dozing pretty soundly when I felt a hand give me a hard shake and Felipe's voice said, "C'mon, Barney, you ain't a private person no more!"

I looked around at the bare field and tried to shake off the tired feeling that made my eyes all gritty. "A *private person?* What's that, Felipe?"

"Guy who ain't with the circus!"

We were directed into our parking place by one of the riggers. As soon as Felipe shut the engine off, he said, "Well, we got to raise the Big Top! Let's go, Barney!"

By the time the Big Top was up, I was just about ready to drop! Lou Beauchamp showed me how to put the rigging up for the fliers, but I was so sleepy I missed most of it.

One bad thing happened when I was up in the top of the arena with Lou, trying to catch on to the rigging. While I was trying to make a line hold fast, somebody shoved me to one side, and I almost fell off the perch.

"You trying to kill somebody?" a harsh voice said. I made a wild grab and caught the wooden section of the platform. Then I found myself looking into the face of Juan del Rio, the young flier.

He was staring at me with hard black eyes, and I

couldn't say a word. He was only sixteen, I found out later, but he looked a lot older. He was as trim as a hawk, as all fliers had to be, and he looked wild—almost vicious, like a hungry wolf. "You make that connection like *that* and I'll fall right on the ground!" he snarled.

Then Lou called out from his perch on the other landing, "Hey, take it easy, Juan. The kid's just learning."

"Let him learn someplace else—cleaning up after the bulls!" Juan shouted, then glared at me. "You watch yourself, rube. I need you like I need a bad ulcer!"

I just tried to hang on, and I felt about as out of place as a crippled bullfrog on the freeway. To tell the truth, I was just about to climb down, collect Jake and Joe, and head back to Cedarville. Then I heard someone say in a soft voice, "Look, Barney, you make this swivel fast to this gusset. See?"

I twisted my head around and saw Angel wearing blue jeans and a plaid shirt. She smiled at me as she put my hands on the lines that had to be fastened. I managed to grin at her. "Yeah, I can see that. Thanks a lot."

"You gonna take in this stray kitten like you always do, Angel?" Juan asked. His sharp black eyes flashed, and he shook his head. "This one will never make it as a rigger." He moved off the platform and slid down the rope like a cat.

Somehow I knew that Juan and I would never be friends. I'd seen the glance he shot at Angel. It said she was his property and look out to anybody who trespassed!

After Angel helped me, Lou taught me the fine points. It was hard, but no harder than learning how to outwait a clever boar coon in the thick wood in the middle of the night. By the time we'd gone through it all slowly, I was pretty sure that with practice I could handle it by myself.

I thought I'd better check up on Jake and Joe, so I wandered around to the cook tent and found Joe sitting down working on a mountain of potatoes.

"Hi, Barney," he said with a grin. "This is Tiny Little. He's going to teach me how to cook, and I'm going to invent him a potato-peeling machine."

Tiny Little couldn't have had a name any more *wrong*. He was about six feet four and must have weighed four hundred pounds. He was so fat that I lost count of his chins, and his stomach fell over his belt like a waterfall. But he had a pleasant red face, and his eyes shone with dignity. He nodded at Joe. "Joe tells me he'll have that machine fixed so that it'll not only *peel* the potatoes, but slice them ready for french fries in no time!"

"If Joe says he can do it, you can bet the farm it'll be done," I said. I gave Joe a quick rub on the head and asked, "You sleepy? I'm just about ready to drop!"

"No, Tiny let me sleep in a little bunk behind his cab all the way."

"Well, I'm going to sack out. Have you seen Jake?"

"He's over with the Joeys, unless he's taking care of stripes."

I stared at him. "What did you say?"

Tiny broke out into a laugh that made his chins ripple. "He said that Jake is with the clowns, unless he's feeding the tiger. Better learn the lingo, Barney. You're part of 'The Greatest Show on Earth' now."

"He'll be over in clown alley, Barney," Joe added. "That's where all the Joeys practice up on their acts."

I made my way out, shaking my head. A kid of ten like Joe got used to things pretty fast, but at my age, it took a little longer to adjust.

Clown alley wasn't hard to find, but Jake wasn't there. Lou was trying to teach a tall, skinny clown with a sad face how to juggle, and he shouted at me. "Jake ain't here, Barney. Try the menagerie tent."

I found Jake near a tall, strong-looking man wearing a pair of riding pants and a white shirt tied with a cord. He was telling Jake, "You have to watch yourself with Rajah." He waved his thick hand toward the huge tiger, who was staring at them with yellow eyes—hungry yellow eyes!

"Is he more dangerous than the lions?" Jake asked.

"Yes! Never forget it!" the trainer said.

I figured he must be Rex Rogers, but he was foreign looking, unlike his name. He had a dark, square face with a clipped mustache and large eyes that never seemed to blink. They were sort of yellow and looked like the tiger's eyes.

"Never get your hand close enough for Rajah to reach, or you'll be minus an arm!"

"But—you let Deidre go into the cage with him," Jake argued.

Then I noticed a girl standing with her back pressed against the tent pole, looking at me with a smile. She was as fair-skinned as Angel was dark, with blue eyes and light honey-colored hair that hung down to her waist. I met her eyes and swallowed—the same old stupid problem: pretty girls stall up my vocal cords!

The trainer glanced at the girl. "Never, unless *I* am there. A tiger is not like other cats. He will pretend to be good for five years. Then he will turn on you and bite your face off in one unguarded second! Never trust a tiger! Never!"

Then Jake saw me. "Hi, Barney. This is Mr. Rex Rogers, and this is his daughter, Deidre."

I nodded and said, "Glad to know you. You all set, Jake?"

"Sure. Joe and I will bunk in with Lou and Heck."

I felt Roger's yellow eyes fixed on me. "You are the older brother?" he asked. "I expect you to keep this one behaving properly. I have discovered that boys have little respect these days. See to it!"

He whirled and stalked off through the door of the

tent—which I thought was pretty impolite. Deidre must have been used to it, though. She moved away from the tent pole and came up closer to give me a smile. "Don't mind Daddy. His bark is worse than his bite."

"Yeah?" Jake grunted and picked up a bucket of meat to take to the next cage. "Well, why don't you tell him I'd rather be *bitten* once in a while than barked at all the time!"

Deidre laughed and said as Jake moved off, "I'm glad you boys have come to help us." She looked up at me. "My, you're tall! That must be nice. I'm so little that I get overlooked by most people."

"Not by guys, I'll bet." That was about the most daring speech I'd ever made to a girl. Since I didn't say something like "Beegie borgie boo"—like I usually did—I tried a few more words. "You really go into the cage with *him?*" I pointed to Rajah.

"Oh, sure," she said with a smile. She had a dimple in each cheek. Somehow I'd never noticed how nice dimples were before, but now it occurred to me that every girl ought to have at least *one*.

"But not without Daddy. I can go in with Simba there. He's just an old softy!" She waved her hand at a huge black-maned lion that was yawning. He showed enough ivory teeth to make a piano keyboard, and I knew it would take ten men and six boys to put me in the same cage with him!

We talked for a few minutes, and she was a really nice girl. I found out that Deidre and the rest of the kids with the circus were in a correspondence school. "I just can't do that old English stuff, Barney!" Deidre said. "It doesn't make any sense, especially those old nouns and adjectives!"

"Well . . ." I cleared my throat and got ready to brag. "You won't have to worry about that, Deidre. It just so happens I'm the very best at English in my whole school!"

"Oh, Barney!" she said with a smile that almost took the enamel off my teeth. "Would you help me with those old themes, please? And call me Dee Dee."

I probably would have helped her hold up Fort Knox if she'd held on to my arm and lifted those big blue eyes up and asked me to!

"Well, I see you're getting acquainted, Barney."

I moved away from Dee Dee, and there was Angel with a funny smile on her face. She looked straight at Dee Dee and said, "I think your father is looking for you."

Dee Dee stared right back. "I'll find him when I need him, Angel." She smiled sweetly. "Barney is going to help me with my English lessons. But you don't need any help with yours, do you, Angel? I mean, you do *so well.*"

Angel ignored her and led me right out of the tent,

saying, "Come on, Barney. Riggers don't have to be bothered with these nasty old animals."

Then I noticed Jake standing there taking it all in. He had a wide grin on his broad face as Angel pulled me out, and he shook his head.

"Barney, I better get you a big stick."

"What for?" I asked, looking over my shoulder.

He waved his hand toward Dee Dee and Angel. "To fight off all these beautiful women that crave your company. But I'll be sure to write Debra and keep her informed."

As Angel pulled me outside, Dee Dee asked, "Who's *Debra?*"

"Just a girl Barney used to know before he got into show biz!" Jake said with a laugh.

By then I was falling-down tired, so I found my way back to Felipe's trailer. I passed by the Cortinas' big trailer and saw Mr. Cortina outside talking to a big man with a red face, the owner of the Cadillac parked close by. They were talking loudly, and Mr. Cortina looked angry. I caught the words ". . . and you will see me in my grave, stone dead, Hunter, before I surrender my circus to you!"

When I stumbled inside, Felipe was making a pot of coffee. He grinned at me. "You better sack out, Barney. You gotta be ready for the Spec pretty soon."

"The *Spec?*"

"Sure. That's the grand parade. I heard Mr. Cortina tell somebody you're supposed to ride one of the bulls from now on. Costume and all."

"Oh." A couple of days ago the idea of dressing up and riding an elephant would have kept me awake for a week. Now it was just another chore. "Felipe, who's the man in the fancy car talking to your brother?"

"Probably Milo Hunter. I saw him pull in an hour ago."

"Who's he? Your brother looked really mad at him."

"Why, I guess he's the villain, Barney." Felipe made a sour face and poured himself some coffee. "You'll find out about it soon enough. Hunter is a big-shot circus owner. He wants to buy up all the small shows like this one and have a monopoly. Looks like he'll do it, too."

"You mean Mr. Cortina will sell to him?"

"Not in ten million years!" Felipe looked angry then. "Thomas is stubborn as a mule, Barney. He'll never sell to Hunter, but that won't matter."

I was pulling off my clothes, longing for that soft bed. "Why not?"

"Because Milo Hunter has the paper on the Cortina Brothers' Circus. That means Thomas borrowed money from him, and now if it's not paid back by the end of this summer, Milo Hunter owns another circus."

I thought about that as I pulled the covers up. "That won't happen will it? I mean, your brother will make enough to pay it off, won't he, Felipe?"

Felipe looked tired then. He set the cup down and gazed sadly out the window. "I don't know, Barney. It would take a miracle, and I guess those are in pretty short supply around here."

He got up and pulled the curtain that separated my bedroom from the rest of the trailer. "If you ever do any praying, Barney, you might put that on your list."

I could tell Felipe didn't have much confidence in prayer, but I said one anyway.

4

The Backyard

THE circus stayed a week in Biloxi, and by Friday all three of us Bucks had gotten into a routine. Joe made Tiny Little's eyes bulge with an invention of his. All you had to do was throw a sack of potatoes into a hopper, and they came out of a chute peeled, sliced, and ready to be cooked in a deep-fat fryer.

"You're a wizard, Joe!" Tiny breathed as the first batch poured out. From then on, Joe was accepted as a full-fledged 'kinker'—a member of the circus. He had the time of his life finding new ways to make the circus equipment better.

Jake, I'm sad to say, was in one of his "scheming" moods. This time he'd gotten Joe involved, and I was afraid they were working on some nutty scheme that would be a disaster. Usually *I* was on the receiving end of the trouble! But everybody liked the two of them, so I felt good about the summer's work.

Every performance was so involved and complicated that the split-second timing confused me for a few days. But then I began to learn how to get the traps to Thomas or to tie back the line from Juan at just the right time. By the end of the week even Juan, who never had many kind words for me, had to admit that I was doing a pretty good job!

The days were different. First, we went to the big tent where Tiny Little and his helpers cooked our meals. And did they do it right! There was always a mountain of eggs, bacon, toast, biscuits, jelly, pancakes, sausage, coffee, tea, and milk for breakfast. Then every night we had a big meal before the performance. Jake made himself a reputation that first week by putting away a record number of pancakes.

After breakfast, I usually wandered into the backyard.

The backyard was like an outdoor living room. Most circus acts come from Europe, so four or five languages besides English were flying around. A lot of the kids went to school during the winter and toured during the summer, but some didn't.

More than school subjects were taught in the backyard. A father would lie on his back juggling his small daughter on his feet, hoping to one day make her part of the act. A mother would lead her six-year-old son up one of the tent's guy ropes, dreaming of the day when he'd be a star of the center ring on the great high wire.

I loved to watch people rehearsing everywhere. Popo the Clown was making his little dog, Sun, jump through a hoop. Juggler Lou was keeping three apples, two bananas, and a rubber ball in the air. Tumblers were turning somersaults and cartwheels.

One tent was just for dressing rooms. The men had one side and the women the other. Trunks stood end to end in long lines, and there was a number on each. Inside were brushes, mirrors, makeup, liniment for aching muscles, and wooden shoes called slop shoes to wear on the many trips between the dressing tent and the Big Top.

As I'd said to Dee Dee about the middle of the week, "It's like one big family." We had been sitting in the backyard with our backs against the tent wall, and I had been helping her diagram sentences. We'd fallen into the habit of meeting every afternoon, and she was doing a good job with her English.

When I'd said the circus was like a family, she'd looked up from her paper and said, "Well, I guess so, but it's not always good."

That surprised me. "But everything is going pretty

well, Dee Dee. Most families don't get along as well as people do here."

She outlined the design on the front of her writing tablet and sighed. "I don't know. *I* don't seem to have many friends."

I almost said, "You would have—if your father wasn't such a *turkey!*" But I didn't. It wouldn't have done any good.

Felipe had told me that Rex Rogers was the meanest guy in the whole circus. He bullied everyone he could and was just plain nasty to one and all. "No wonder that girl of his is lonesome!" Felipe had said. "That old man of hers keeps people's backs up all the time."

I'd had a taste of that when her father stopped once when I was trying to show Dee Dee the difference between a noun clause and an adverb clause. Our heads were a little close together, but you would've thought I was trying to convert her to *communism* the way Rex Rogers reacted!

"You! Boy!" He acted like he didn't know my name all the time, and that gave me a fit. "No work to do? I will inform Thomas. Maybe you won't have time to lollygag around young girls! Deidre, get yourself to the trailer!"

A real *prince,* this Rex Rogers!

I saw the tears fill Dee Dee's eyes, but she obeyed like a whipped puppy.

Felipe, who had been close by taking it all in, came

over and plopped down beside me. "Don't take it so personal, Barney. You're nothing special. I mean, Rogers is nasty to everybody. If I had to say it, he'd be my choice for the Phantom."

I stared at him. *"The phantom?* What's *that?"*

"Oh, it's just a silly ghost story about the circus." He shrugged his shoulders. "Remember that old movie, *The Phantom of the Opera?"*

"Yeah, I saw it on TV. About the guy who gets his face all burned at the opera and hangs around haunting it. That the one?"

"That's it. Well, about ten years ago a flier named Manuel Delgado fell and was killed. The story goes that he fell because somebody sabotaged his rigging; so he comes back as a spook and causes accidents. Now, whenever an accident happens, circus people say, 'The Phantom of the Big Top did it.' Lots of them even claim to have seen him. But circus people are awfully superstitious!"

"You don't believe in this phantom, do you, Felipe?"

"Of course not! But in anything as complicated as a circus, you're going to have foul-ups. Any equipment will break down. But lately, we've had too many bad breaks! For instance, a truck broke loose and smashed into the cook tent last week. Nobody got hurt, but it messed Tiny up so much that we had to eat store-bought grub for two or three days."

"Are you saying those things weren't accidental?" I asked.

He shrugged and got up to leave. "I don't know, Barney. I'm just a clown. But as long as I've been with the circus, I've never seen as much hard luck hit so often as it has around us for the past month." Then his face got hard, and he looked in the direction where Rex Rogers had disappeared. "And if there *is* a phantom, I'd vote for *him* as the most likely suspect!"

Later that afternoon as I was going over the webbing, I asked Angel about what Felipe had said. We were pretty good friends by then, so I just came right out with what I thought. "Angel, all that talk about a phantom— I think that's just superstition. Circus people are pretty simple. So if a few bad things happened, that's who they'd blame it on."

She was pulling at the safety net and suddenly caught hold of it and flipped herself up without any effort. Then she came down again light as a feather and stood beside me. She put her hand on my arm and gave me that smile that made jelly out of my bones. "Barney, do you think I'm as pretty as Dee Dee?"

For a minute I just stood there. Sometimes girls irritated me. Here I was talking about important stuff, and then, out of the blue, Angel changed the subject. I hated it when people did that!

"What? Oh, sure I do!" I said, trying to ignore the way

she kept leaning on me and fiddling with the button on my collar. "But about this ghost. You know what I think? I think it's just carelessness—that's what! A rope breaks because it's old and nobody replaced it. And when a truck breaks loose and smashes something, it's because somebody didn't set the brakes right. So this ghost stuff is silly!"

"Do you think I'm as pretty as Debra?"

She hadn't heard a word I'd said! So I just said, "Come on, Angel. Let's go get something to eat."

"No, let me show you how to fall into the net," she said with a giggle. "If you want to be a kinker, you have to know a little about every act."

She pulled at me, and we went up the ladder. She could go up the ropes easily enough, but it still was a problem for me to get up on that high platform. Finally we were up on the perch where the fliers rested between jumps.

"Now, let's see you fall into the net," she said with a mischievous smile.

It was only about twenty feet down from that first perch, but it looked far when I glanced down. "I don't want to, Angel," I said, then added, "It's too *easy!*"

She grinned at me. "You think so, Barney? Do you know that circus kids who want to do trapeze acts spend *months* just learning how to fall into the net?"

"What's there to learn? You just fall!"

She laughed. "And you just break your neck! If you don't fall just right, that's what can happen."

"There's the net!" I pointed down. "It'll catch me, won't it?"

She stopped smiling. "If you hit on the edge of it, or it threw you off, you'd be dead! Watch, Barney."

She stood on the edge of the platform and with a little jump fell toward the net. It looked easy. Then she made a full turn, striking the net with her shoulders first and letting the tension of the net throw her up after she'd hit. She bounded to a standing position and smiled up at me. "Now, *you* try it, Barney. Just fall forward and hit with your shoulders and back."

Well, there it was. What I really *wanted* to do was to crawl down the ladder one careful step at a time. But Angel had just done something, and now if I said I was afraid to, I'd look pretty bad. At least, I thought I would.

So I edged to the front of the platform and stared down at the net, which seemed to be farther and farther away all the time. Then I took a deep breath and decided that no girl was going to outdo Barney Buck! I leaned over and fell into the net.

Actually it was a little like going off the bluff in the catapult Joe had invented to launch kids into the Caddo River. The world sort of went around in a circle and I felt dizzy, but then I felt the net on my back and it shot me right up into the air again! I lost my balance and bounced around, but I had done it!

"Wonderful, Barney!" Angel cried. I looked down. Her dark eyes were bright, and she was clapping her hands. "Now, once more!"

For an hour I kept climbing up and falling into the net, and it got to be pretty easy! I was seeing myself as some great acrobat when I did something wrong. Maybe I didn't duck my head quick enough. Anyway, when I hit, I was off balance, and the net threw me to one side. Angel screamed, and I knew I was coming down very close to the edge of the safety net! I felt the rope along the edge catch my right shoulder and flip me over so quickly I had time to make only one wild grab with my left hand. I was glad I caught the net. Otherwise I would've landed head-first on the hard clay ground.

I hung there by one hand, feeling like a real fool. Suddenly Mr. Cortina's voice boomed out, "Wonderful! Wonderful, Barney!" Then I let go and fell.

When I got up, Mr. Cortina came over and began to pat me on the shoulder. "That was very good!"

My stomach was still churning over the close call, and I just stared at him. *"Good?* I nearly knocked my brains out!"

He gave Angel a smile and said, "Ah, but you didn't, and that shows you have the one thing an acrobat must have that he cannot learn by practice!"

"What's that?"

"Reaction!" Mr. Cortina grinned. "You caught that net by pure reaction, Barney. Ah, my boy, too bad you're so old! You would have made a great acrobat!"

"Hey, I'm not old!" I protested.

"Yes, for an acrobat, you are very old," he said with a slow shake of his head. "You must begin when you are six—even younger." Then he smiled and said to Angel, "He will never be a flier, but he is *good,* no?"

"Yes, Papa," Angel said with a smile. "Maybe we can make him a catcher?"

"He's too tall for *that!*" Mr. Cortina laughed. "But it is good you are giving him some feel for life under the Big Top. Just don't let him try a triple unless I am there to catch him! All right, my little one?"

"All right, Papa." Angel laughed. "And he is very good at diagramming sentences for English!"

That became a joke among Mr. Cortina, Angel, and me. He'd say, "Well, are you ready for the triple, Barney?" and I'd say, "No, Mr. Cortina, but are you ready to diagram a complex sentence?" Then he would roar with laughter.

Angel did teach me a lot of simple stuff about the trapeze. I even got over my fear of heights long enough to swing from the traps way up high in the Big Top. Not that I would ever turn loose of that bar the way Angel did. But I *pretended* to, just like a guy pretending to be a home-run hitter for the Yankees or a basketball star dunking a shot for the NBA.

I couldn't see any harm in it. Besides, Angel and I had become good friends. What I *didn't* know was that Jake was taking this all in and making his Master Plan to make me a star of the "Greatest Show on Earth"!

If I'd known that, I would've run back to Goober Holler for dear life!

5
The Phantom Strikes!

BY the time we left Biloxi and moved to Ruston, Louisiana, I had gotten the rigging down pat. Lou kept waiting for me to make a mistake, but finally he said, "Kid, you're a genuine rigger!" He must have said something like that to Mr. Cortina, because from then on he just seemed to assume that the traps and all the rigging would be safe.

"I wish I could learn out of books as quick as you learned rigging, Barney," Angel said with a sigh one day. "I just can't understand all this old *literature!* I don't see any sense in it anyway."

"What book is it?" I asked. We were standing under the trapeze watching Juan and Mr. Cortina practice a new stunt. I was impressed over how easy they made it look.

"An old book named *Call of the Wild*. It's silly! Who wants to read about a dog?" She pouted. Most people look dumb when they pout, but Angel looked . . . well, pretty good!

"Actually, I don't think it's about a dog," I said. "We read that last year in literature class. Oh, I know there's a dog in the story, but it's actually about how people act."

"Really!" Angel edged closer and put her hand over mine. "You're so *smart,* Barney! Listen, why don't you meet me tonight after supper, and you can teach me all about this stuff? It would really make Mama and Papa happy if I could do better. Will you, pleeeze?"

I could resist anything except pancakes and pretty girls saying "pleeeze"! "Well, I was supposed to help Dee Dee with her grammar, but—"

"You can do that later. Now you come to our trailer right after supper, all right?"

Juan had flown through the air, and after Mr. Cortina had him, he'd dropped into the net just in time to hear Angel ask me to their trailer.

He flipped off the net and wiped the sweat from his brow. "You forget we were going to catch the late movie in town tonight, Angel?"

"Oh, Juan, I'm sorry! But I'm doing so bad with my lessons. Papa, don't you think it would be all right for

Barney to help me with my homework tonight? He's really good in English!"

"Sure," Mr. Cortina said, giving her a squeeze. "You take all the help you can get, sweetheart."

I was looking at Juan. He smiled a lot, but just for a second he let that smile fall. If there was ever an angry look, he had it! Then he just walked away.

That was the one big problem I was having. Juan never said anything to me in front of Mr. Cortina, but he put me down all the time in front of everybody else, especially Angel. He'd talk about how clumsy I was and how I didn't know anything. Both were true, but he made that all seem much worse than it actually was.

He wasn't the only one. Dee Dee's dad, Rex Rogers, had taken a dislike to all of us Bucks. He made it clear that he didn't want his daughter contaminated by us. He was a difficult man, and Dee Dee was so afraid of him that she trembled when he gave her a glance.

All the other people laughed at us Bucks because we made so many dumb mistakes, but it was a good kind of laughter, and I didn't mind. But Rex Rogers and Juan del Rio were downright spiteful. They got at Joe and Jake a little, but I got most of it, and it was getting me down.

Maybe it was because I wasn't very good at anything much, except maybe for hunting with my black-and-tan hound, Tim, and diagramming sentences. I was so tall that it made me sort of clumsy, although Coach Little-john said that in another year or two I would fill out and get coordinated. I spent a lot of time worrying about that, besides my being red-headed and shaped like a stork!

I had tried to listen when Coach had said, "You're made exactly the way God designed you, Barney. When you find fault with the way you look, you're faulting God himself." I tried to think about that a lot, and it helped.

Still, everybody at the circus could do something first-class. Maybe I had listened to Juan del Rio and Rex Rogers too much. That was why, when Jake and Joe came to me with their scheme, I went along with it. Jake must've had some kind of radar that picked up when I was ripe for falling for his dumb ideas. He always caught me just when I was too weak to resist!

Jake had been hatching something ever since we'd left Cedarville. He sprang it on me behind the midway on my way to the trailer, and I saw by the light in his eyes that I was about to be introduced to his latest brainstorm.

"What is it this time, Jake? I know it's going to make us rich and famous—like the last *thirty* times you had a plan."

He didn't even blush. "You've got it, Barney. This can't miss! I personally guarantee this is going to put us in the upper-income bracket, and your name will be on the program. Never fear—Jake is here!"

I looked at Joe. "And I suppose you're in on it, too?"

"Sure I am, Barney! It's my invention."

"All right, let's have it." I sighed and sat down.

Joe handed Jake a canvas sack, and Jake held it before my eyes. "This is the baby, Barney. Feast your eyes." He opened the sack and pulled out a long piece of what looked like rope.

"Why, this looks like that rubber tubing you made that fool catapult out of, Joe," I said, taking a closer look. All it had was a type of harness at one end and what looked like a pulley at the other end.

"Sure, Barney. I had lots of this cable left over, so I brought it along."

"Well, what *is* it?"

Jake stroked the cable proudly and said, "Why, this is the Magic Yo-Yo! And you're going to be the first acrobat in the world to become the Human Yo-Yo! Isn't that a kick in the head, Barney?"

I just stared at him. "I'm going to do *what?*"

"I know it sounds wild, Barney," Joe said. "But actually it's easy! Look, you see this wheel on this end? Well, that just slips over the high wire. And it can't come loose. See how this part slips down and locks?"

I nodded and picked up the webbing on the other end. "And I guess I put this on, right?"

"Sure, just like a parachute harness. You couldn't fall out, even if you wanted to," Joe said. "What you do is clamp this wheel over the high wire. Then you scoot out a few feet to get away from the pole that holds the tent up. Then all you do is just fall."

"That's all, is it? Just fall fifty feet into the net?"

"Oh, you don't use a net!" Jake waved his hand at the suggestion. "The idea is that you go down until the Magic Yo-Yo catches you, and you just go *boing, boing, boing!* Up and down like a yo-yo. Now isn't that great?" He smiled and waited for me to brag on him.

I just looked at him. "All I can figure out, Jake, is that you're tired of having an older brother. You're doing this so you won't have to fool with ol' Barney anymore. Am I right?"

Jake looked hurt, but Joe said, "I know it looks that way, Barney, but actually it's a lot safer than the Solar-cycle." (That was a sort of hang glider powered by solar cells that Joe had dreamed up for me to fly.) "Jake's right. You can't fall out of the harness, and the pulley can't come off the wire. But it'll *look* real dangerous! You head right for the ground, see, and the whole audience gives that holler like when one of the acrobats slips. You just touch the ground and then go way back up again! Oh, you'll be *something,* Barney! And I'll bet everybody in the circus will really be proud of you!"

Both of them could have talked all night and gotten nowhere. But when Joe said, "Everybody in the circus will be proud of you!" a thrill went right down my spine.

I could almost hear the crowd cheering already: "Barney Buck—the Human Yo-Yo!"

That would show that ol' Rex Rogers and Juan del Rio! I thought with a smile. "OK, gimme that thing and I'll think about it—maybe test it out a little. But don't say a word, you hear? I don't want this to get out until I'm sure it'll work."

They both promised, and I thought there was a fair chance Jake would keep his mouth shut, especially when I agreed that he'd get a third of the fortune we were going to make out of the act. Any time high places were involved, Jake turned green and Joe fainted. I wasn't a lot better, but as Jake always put it, I was the oldest!

After the show that night, I went over to the Cortinas' trailer. Angel and I talked about things while her father sat in front of a big desk working with Lou Beauchamp on bills and stuff. Mrs. Cortina didn't look like a famous trapeze artist. She had on gold-rimmed glasses and was sewing under a big reading lamp.

I found out that Angel hadn't read *Call of the Wild,* so for a couple of hours I read parts of it and told the rest. Then I began telling her what I thought it all meant, and we got so interested that neither one of us noticed that the three grown-ups had stopped their work and were listening.

"Look, Angel, when you write your theme about this

book, you got to tell about how the author, Jack London, had a real adventurous life. How he was on the gold rush to the Klondike and fought with pirates and was a newspaper reporter who traveled all over the world. Then he got real rich as a writer. And in this book, you have to see how he got sort of disgusted with the world. That's what the dog does—the husky named Buck!"

"I don't understand what a dog has to do with people!" She frowned. "Why doesn't he just say what he means?"

I laughed at her. "Well, that's what preachers do on Sunday. They just come right out and tell people what they want them to hear. But I guess writers don't do that. See, this dog Buck lives in the South, but he gets stolen and they take him to the gold rush in Alaska. And he nearly starves to death, because he's such a nice dog."

"Why is that?" she asked, her eyes getting bigger.

"Because Buck never had to fight for anything in the South. But in the gold rush days, they just threw fish to the dogs, and the strongest dogs got the most fish. If a dog didn't cheat or steal to get more fish, he starved."

"Well, that's *mean!*"

"Sure, but I guess Jack London thought the world was like that. He says right here that just when Buck was about to starve to death, he finally stole a fish—and from then on, he took whatever he had to in order to live. So, what you have to say in your paper is that Jack London believed men do all kinds of bad things to live and the weak don't make it."

"That book says that?" The question made me jump a little, because I'd forgotten the adults. Mr. Cortina was sitting there with some papers in his hand. "I didn't know the books Angel was reading taught things like that—that you have to be *bad* to live. I don't want her to read that book."

Lou looked at him. "You don't want her to know how things really are, Thomas? Maybe it's better she learns that some men and women are like animals. Maybe if she learns it from a book, she won't get caught for real by one of them."

"I think that may be true, Thomas," Mrs. Cortina said with a nod. She had taken her glasses off and was staring at Angel. "As long as she knows that not *all* people are like that." Then she dimpled up, just like Angel, and added, "But she has such a good teacher that I'm sure he will not let that happen!"

"That is true." Mr. Cortina smiled. "Your Sunday school teacher says you are a real fine Christian boy. That is good. We go to church again Sunday, OK?" Then he frowned at the paper in his hand.

Lou caught the look and gave a bitter smile. "That Milo Hunter—*he's* one who takes what he likes, Thomas. He's like that dog Buck in the book."

"Yes, but it is my fault. I borrowed the money. He has the right to claim my circus if I cannot pay." Then Mr. Cortina looked at me and smiled sadly. "You say your prayers, Barney? I know you do. Better put in a good strong one for the Cortina Brothers' Circus. If just one thing breaks down, it will be the Milo Hunter Circus."

Well, nobody felt much like talking after that. I was about to leave when I said, "Hey, I'll bet God is going to let you keep your circus, Mr. Cortina. The Bible says if you have faith as big as a mustard seed, you can say to a mountain, 'Get out of here!' and it'll go!"

He was real tired, but he came over and put a hand on my shoulder. "Barney, I'm a pretty bad example as a Christian, so I guess you'll have to have the faith for me, all right?"

I gulped and said, "Sure, Mr. Cortina," and then left. I felt he was putting it all on *me,* and I'd never won any prizes for my prayers. That was for sure! But I made up my mind if my little prayer was worth anything, Thomas Cortina would have it!

It was after ten, and most of the circus folks went to bed early, but I didn't go to Felipe's trailer. I picked up the Magic Yo-Yo from the spot where I'd hidden it behind the hay. Rajah glared at me with yellow eyes and rumbled in his chest, but there was only a single light overhead, and nobody was stirring. I knew one of the men would check the animals about midnight, but I'd be finished long before that.

It was dark under the Big Top and quiet. I thought about the chances of a ghost haunting the circus, and the hair on my neck stood up as I made my way to the center ring. It was so quiet I could hear my own footsteps on the packed earth, and the rigging squeaked as I climbed to the top of the platform.

I felt scared to the bone as I clamped the pulley with the wheel onto the wire, then shoved it as far out as I could. My hands were trembling as I strapped on the harness, and when I stood up and looked down, the ground looked about a mile away. The net was still up, so I knew that even if something went wrong with the harness, I'd be all right. I was sure glad that Angel had been teaching me how to fall in that net, though!

I'd been finding out that the longer you look at something scary, the worse it gets, so I just made myself step off that platform, and down I went! I fell only about ten feet before I felt the harness tighten, but then I just kept falling. The net was rushing up at me, and I knew that I wasn't supposed to hit the net with my feet, but it was too late to roll over and hit on my back!

Then my feet touched the net, but the cable had stretched as far as it would go. All of a sudden I was jerked back into the air. It took my breath, and my plan to go back up gracefully came to nothing. I was jerked up with my arms flailing and my legs pumping like crazy. Then my head tapped the wire, and down I came again.

I kept bobbing up and down like a yo-yo and was glad no one was there to see me. Finally I was able to get some control, and suddenly it was *fun!*

The wheel was slipping on the wire, but that made no difference, I would dip down, then pop back up again. As I got the hang of it, I learned how to keep my legs and arms under control. Actually, I could see how a real acrobat could go on this thing—somersaults and all!

Stopping and getting off was the main problem. I thought I'd have to hang there until morning and get pulled down like an apple off a tree or something. But somehow I managed to swing until I caught the ladder going up the pole, and I made it. I knew the thing was going to work, but it would take a lot of practice. Someone would have to rig a line to the pulley and pull me along the wire. I couldn't bob around in one spot.

Suddenly someone called out, "Barney!" and I nearly jumped out of my skin. I whirled around and saw Dee Dee coming out of the shadows.

"Dee Dee!" I said with a big sigh of relief. "I thought for sure the Phantom had me! Don't ever sneak up on me like that again!"

"I wasn't sneaking. I came to check the cats, and I

heard the rigging squeak. What in the world are you doing?"

I had to tell her the whole story, of course. She listened, and a smile lit up her face. "I'll help you, Barney! It'll be fun. It'll be our secret!"

"Well, I do need somebody to pull the Magic Yo-Yo along the wire, but I thought maybe I'd ask Angel since she's used to being up high."

"No, *I'll* do it," Dee Dee said at once. "And we'll meet here every night at this time. I have to come to check the animals, and that'll work out just right. So we'll do it, OK? Oh, won't they be surprised when you do your act for the first time!"

I agreed to do it. I *did* need some help, and she had to be there anyway. I walked Dee Dee back to her trailer and headed for Felipe's.

I tried not to make any noise as I opened the door, but it squeaked as always. I stopped and held my breath, but I guess Felipe had gone to sleep. He went to bed real early every night, and that made my plan easier to follow. I got into bed and lay there for awhile, thinking of how great it was going to be when I had my own act in the circus!

About ten or fifteen minutes later, I jumped right on to the floor. Somebody was shouting outside, and lights were going on all over the lot.

I scrambled into my clothes. Felipe and I got in

each other's way getting through the door. "It's a fire!" he said. I followed him as he ran toward the Big Top.

A blaze was leaping up and throwing crazy-looking shadows over the big tent. I remembered Felipe telling me of the Ringling Brothers' Circus burning down in 1944, killing 168 people!

As I got inside the tent, I saw a bunch of men beating the blaze that was around the hay where I'd hidden the Magic Yo-Yo. One section of the canvas was burning, but that was pretty well under control, thanks to a water hose held by Lou.

My heart was really pounding, and everybody else was shaken up, too. Nearly everybody in the circus was watching the smoldering hay.

Lou looked around and said, "We were lucky. Another five minutes and there wouldn't have been an inch of canvas left—and maybe some of us would have gotten burned up, too."

Mr. Cortina was pale as a sheet. "How did it start?"

"That Phantom!" somebody whispered, and a murmur went up from the crowd.

"No! This was no phantom!" he cried. "It takes fire to start a fire. Somebody had to drop a match! Who was the last one in here?"

"I guess it was you, wasn't it, Barney?"

Every head turned to stare at me, and I saw a little

glint in Juan's eyes as he spoke. "Didn't I see you come out of the tent a few minutes ago?"

Then Felipe spoke up, and I knew he wasn't trying to pin the blame on me the way Juan was. "Sure, you came in just a few minutes before it was discovered. Did you see anybody?"

I just stood there, and the silence got pretty thick. Then Mr. Cortina said, "Barney, what were you doing here at that time of night?"

"He was—" Dee Dee started to answer, but I cut her off. If Rex Rogers ever found out that his daughter had been out alone with me in the middle of the night, he'd probably beat us both to death.

"I was just working with the rigging," I said. It sounded pretty lame even to me. People were looking at each other, and several of them whispered and shook their heads.

Mr. Cortina stared at me, then finally shrugged and said, "Well, perhaps it was an accident. Some rube might have flipped a cigarette into the hay, and it smoldered until it caught fire."

"No cigarette smolders for four hours, Thomas!" Rex Rogers said loudly. "And it wasn't a ghost. I think Buck has some explaining to do."

Dee Dee started to speak, but I gave her a shake of my head. All I could say was, "I was in the rigging, and I didn't see anybody lighting any fires."

The circus people had been very good to me and my

brothers, but I could see that they were suddenly on guard. They were close-knit and they really didn't know anything about us Bucks.

Mr. Cortina noticed what was happening and said, "All right, go to bed. I'll take care of this."

Everyone filed out, muttering and talking. Some of them had marked me down as guilty. Angel and her mother didn't.

"Don't worry, Barney, it'll be all right," Felipe said with a smile.

"Do you think I did it, Felipe?"

"No, I don't, Barney."

"Well, I know I didn't—and if I didn't, then who did? And why?"

He put his arm around my shoulder. "Barney, I got my suspicions. But it takes proof for a thing like this. Let's you and me keep our eyes open. I got a feeling that this phantom puts on his pants one leg at a time, just like the rest of us. And if we don't get him soon, he's gonna maybe get some of us."

"But people think *I* set the fire!"

"You'll just have to show 'em different, Barney. And the best way to do that is catch him right in the act."

We went to bed, but I didn't sleep until nearly morning. I had dreams of a ghost who kept setting fire to me, and when I pulled his mask off, it was *me* under there. Thank goodness I never put much stock in dreams, anyway!

6

The Human Yo-Yo

BARNEY, you gotta snap out of it," Jake said. "If you don't stop acting like a sick cat, you *will* get sick. Now eat up and don't worry so much about that ol' phantom!"

"Yeah, I guess you're right, Jake," I said, forcing myself to take a bite of stew. "But everybody treats me like I was under suspicion for murder!"

"No, they don't," he argued. "Just some of them— mostly that mangy lion trainer and that Juan guy. You're just imagining most of it."

I knew he was right, but it had been a miserable week since the fire. Rex Rogers had forbidden his daughter to speak to me, Juan hadn't missed a chance to go over every bit of rigging I had worked on, and even Mr. Cortina seemed a little uncomfortable around me. There hadn't been any more accidents, but Felipe had said, "Don't let your guard down, Barney. We ain't through yet."

"You think it's Rex Rogers, don't you?" I asked.

He gave me a narrow glance. "I'm not naming a name right now. All I'm saying is he could have set that fire as well as anybody. He goes right by there a dozen times a day, and sometimes late at night. He was close by when some of the other 'accidents' happened, too. I ain't saying a word until . . ." Then he clamped his jaw shut and walked off, but I knew where he stood.

I was just about to get up when Mr. Cortina stopped by our table and said, "Barney, I got a call from Coach Littlejohn this morning. Some of your friends from Cedarville are driving down to catch the show Friday."

"Hey, that's when we do our Independence Day show, ain't it, Thomas?" Lou said around a huge mouthful of mashed potatoes. He was so short he had to sort of hook his chin over the table. "Yeah, that's the Fourth, all right. You'll see something then, all you Bucks. You better have something ready."

"What do you mean by that, Lou?" Jake asked.

"Oh, the Fourth, it's a big day for circus people." Lou laughed. "In the morning we put a show on for *us*. Everybody has to do an act, but not his regular act. Like the acrobats have to put on a clown act, or maybe the bareback riders have to do a high-wire bit. Stuff like that. Then we always have a baseball game right under the Big Top at the end."

"Oh, it's fun!" Angel said, smiling at me. "I'm really expecting something good from you, Barney, and you boys, too."

I just nodded, but after Jake got me alone, he said, "Barney, I think the Independence Day show they're talking about would be a good time for us to put on our Human Yo-Yo act."

"It's always *us,* but where are you when I'm dangling up there?"

"Why, I'm with you in spirit, Barney, you know that!" Jake grinned. "Well, will you do it? Coach and Debra will be here to watch. Wouldn't they think you were something?"

That brother of mine knew how to hook me! I found myself nodding, and the more I thought about it, the better I liked it. A couple of times, I managed to practice when nobody else was around. Nobody paid much attention to me anyway, since I was always messing around with the rigging.

By the time Friday rolled around, I felt pretty sure I was going to be a hit. Early that morning, Coach, Uncle Dave, and Debra pulled up in Coach's Camaro. I had the feeling that somebody, maybe Jake himself, had written to tell the Coach how punk I was feeling, and so they'd come to cheer me up.

We all hollered and shook hands and stuff, but Debra didn't say much. Actually she talked more to Jake and Joe than she did to *me*. The more standoffish she was, the more awkward I felt. So *I* held off.

But there was a lot going on. The cook tent was decorated with red, white, and blue bunting, and the band was playing songs like "Yankee Doodle Dandy" and "America" as hard as they could.

Then we went inside the Big Top. Lou had said nobody would do his own act, and he was right. It was funny to see a couple of clowns trying to do a trapeze act, and then even funnier to see Thomas and Lillian Cortina trying to ride a pair of unicycles, falling down off their one-wheelers and sprawling like a couple of kids!

There was a lot of imitating and teasing, and everybody was laughing and having a great time. One of the funniest things was toward the end. They set up the big cage in the center ring, and Simba, the big black-maned lion, came out of the chute. Felipe took a whip and a chair and acted like a lion trainer. When Simba roared and swiped at him, he'd fall flat on the seat of his pants or run to hide behind the bars.

Uncle Dave stared at that. "That feller's gonna get killed!"

I laughed and showed off what I'd learned. "No, that lion wouldn't hurt a fly, Uncle Dave. He looks like a killer, but Dee Dee cleans his teeth with a toothbrush and he just purrs. See, they didn't even put the roof on the cage he's so tame."

"You could have fooled me," Coach said. He went slightly pale under his dark tan. "I wouldn't get in that cage for a million dollars."

Then there were lots of games. The grown-ups pushed peanuts with their noses and ran in potato-sack and three-legged races. Finally Mr. Cortina got up and said, "Folks, we're going to play our baseball game after this next act. Jake Buck tells me that he and his brothers have a special act. Let's have a big hand for . . . the Buck Brothers!"

Everybody started laughing. Jake was grinning like an idiot and holding out the Magic Yo-Yo. I got up, my face red as my hair, wishing that Joe and Jake were interested in flower growing or something that wouldn't get me into messes like this.

"Oh, I didn't know you were a performer, Barney," Coach chuckled. "Well, break a leg. That's what show biz folks say to someone just going on."

"You go show 'em how a Goober Holler man can do it, Barney!" Uncle Dave yelped. I stumbled down to where Jake and Joe were grinning at me.

Jake took over as announcer while I took the harness

and started climbing to the top of the pole. I got up there, and Jake was bragging about how I was the wonder of the world—the Human Yo-Yo!

I got the harness on and clamped the pulley onto the wire. Then I heard Angel call out, "Barney! We better pull the cage down and put up the net!"

"No need for that!" Jake said loudly. "The daring Human Yo-Yo works *without* a net. Now watch, ladeeeeez and gents, as Barney Buck, the one and only Human Yo-Yo, defies death!"

Mr. Cortina and Lou hollered at the same time for me not to move. I guess they'd seen what I was up to, and they didn't want me to get hurt. But I was all ready to go, and then I put a little something extra into my act, something I'd already dreamed up.

I stood on the edge, then made out I was losing my balance. I started windmilling my arms around and began hollering, "Oh! I'm falling!" I stepped off still waving my arms and screaming.

Those circus folks had been bringing fans up out of their seats for years, but this time *they* were the ones who jumped up and screamed!

I heard Debra scream above all the rest, and I kind of liked that. It served her right for not appreciating me! Nobody was going to forget the Human Yo-Yo for a long time!

Of course, after I made my first bounce, they all

caught on—the circus people, anyway. When people spend their lives fooling other people, they really get a kick out of it when somebody is able to fool them. They all started laughing as I bobbed up and down inside the cage. My feet would just touch the ground—I'd practiced for that one—and then I'd fly up and go about as high as the wire. Sometimes I'd be touching it with my head.

The whole tent was just rocking with people laughing, and of course I was really feeling good. I was getting a little dizzy, because I'd never gone so long on the Magic Yo-Yo.

All at once, I heard a scream. It got so quiet it was scary! Then there was a lot of hollering and screaming that I couldn't understand.

I thought some kid had fallen off the seats or something. It never occurred to me they were all screaming because of *me* until I began falling back down toward the ground. When I looked up, there was Rajah, yellow eyes gleaming, teeth like knives, coming across the cage right at me!

I didn't have time to wonder *how* he'd gotten into the chute and into the big cage. I let my feet hit the ground, and I shoved off as hard as I could. The cable yanked me up just as he made a big jump. The muscles under his stripes moved like steel, and his claws looked like a bunch of sharp, glittering swords—all aimed right at my throat.

I flew up just in time, and there was a cry of relief—
but I was already worried about coming back down!

I tried to catch the wire overhead but missed it, and
down I went to where Rajah had turned around, looking for his "breakfast." When I hit not two feet in front
of his nose, he jumped straight up in the air and
roared!

I kept popping up and down, and Rajah kept looking
at where I'd been. I threw myself around so I would hit
in a different spot each time. I hoped the pulley would
slide back toward the cage, but I was really moving out
toward the center.

Rajah'll get me sooner or later, I thought. I felt dizzy,
then noticed his yellow eyes beginning to follow me as I
went up. Suddenly I came down right on his head! I felt
the impact clear through my tennis shoes, and it scared
me spitless!

All the time this was happening, I heard people
screaming for Rex Rogers. If he didn't come and get
that monster out of the cage, I was a goner. But there
wasn't any sign of him.

Everything was getting pretty blurry, when the the
crowd shouted, "No! Don't do it, Dee Dee!" At about the
same time I heard Lillian Cortina scream, "Angel!" And
she wasn't a screaming woman.

I was too dizzy to see what happened next. They told
me about it later. Dee Dee had gone to the door of the

cage and stepped inside, picking up a little chair her
father used. Then she called to the tiger.

"Rajah! Here!"

At the same time Angel had climbed to the platform
and picked up one of the nylon ropes tied there. She'd
walked out on the wire as pretty as you please, bent
over, and looped the rope around the pulley. Then she'd
gone back to the perch, and while Dee Dee kept Rajah
busy, she'd pulled me back down the wire until I felt the
cage wall.

I tried to stop bobbing up and down, and by some
miracle had managed to crawl outside the cage where
Heck Rawlings, the strong man, jumped up and got me
down. He pulled the harness off, and I wobbled around
like a baby.

Finally the world stopped spinning. I saw Rajah heading down the chute and Dee Dee coming out the steel
door. Someone tried to grab her, and Angel slid off the
perch to the ground.

I felt like a dog! Because of me, those two girls had
risked their lives.

Finally it got all sorted out. Mr. Cortina made a long
speech about how many times in the history of the
circus performers had risked life and limb for a fellow
performer. Some had actually died, he said, and he was
proud to see that this part of the circus was not dead!
Then he reached down and picked up Angel. Heck

picked up Dee Dee, and you could have heard the cheers back in Cedarville!

A baseball game would have been pretty tame after that! When we all broke up, Mr. Cortina told me and my brothers to come to his trailer.

Coach, Uncle Dave, and Debra were there and looked pretty pale. I must have been a funny sight— my dumb freckles jumping out like flags.

Coach was the first to speak. "Barney, you ought to be horsewhipped! That was a fool stunt! Pack your bag!"

I gulped and tears started to fill my eyes, but I clamped my jaw shut and blinked them back. "Yes sir."

"Now just a minute, Dale," Uncle Dave said. "Maybe this whole thing wasn't as bad as it looked. Mr. Cortina, I'd like to hear what you've got to say."

"It was almost a tragedy," he said and bit his lip. "But if the cat had not gotten into the ring, it would have been all right. I think the boys have shown a good spirit. The yo-yo thing—well, Barney, you must not do it again. You don't realize how dangerous it is. It looks simple, but you could break your neck with that thing."

"Well, I won't break *my* neck!" Lou had come along with us, and he had a big grin on under his paint. "It's the best idea for a clown act I've seen in many a day!"

"Clown act?" Mr. Cortina asked.

"Sure, Thomas. Can't you see me and Freddy

bobbing up and down with that ol' pussycat of a lion swiping at us? It'd have the customers out of their seats!"

Mr. Cortina stroked his chin, a light beginning to appear in his eyes. "That may be a good idea. . . ."

"Good? It's *great!*" Lou shouted. "And we could have a boxing match, bobbing up and down missing each other! And a lot of things I've already got in mind."

Jake stepped forward. "Maybe you'd like to talk money, Lou. The Magic Yo-Yo is *my* idea!"

Jake's comments didn't surprise me. Suddenly everybody started laughing. Lou waddled up to Jake and looked up at him. "Sure we'll pay you for the Magic Yo-Yo—at the end of the summer. Come on and we'll go talk terms."

"You better watch that boy." Uncle Dave grinned as Jake and Lou left. "He'll have the gold fillings out of your teeth!"

There was more talk, but finally Mr. Cortina convinced Coach that we should stay. Mr. Cortina looked at Dee Dee and Angel. "Why, you can't take Barney away from his class," he said. "He gives up all his free time every night to teach these young ladies English."

Uncle Dave gave Debra a glance. She was staring at the two girls, and I didn't know what she was thinking. I usually never did. Then Uncle Dave said, "Well, now I think that's real nice of Barney. Don't you think so, Debra?"

She gave me a funny look, then glanced at those two girls and finally at me.

"I think it's just peachy keen!" she said between gritted teeth. "Take me home, Grandpa!" Then she sailed out with her nose in the air.

Why couldn't girls be as easy to get along with as black-and-tan hounds?

7

Jake's Brainstorm

WELL, *one* good thing came out of the Human Yo-Yo act, Barney. Even if you never do it again, nobody suspects you of being the Phantom!"

Felipe was trying to learn how to balance a long stick on his nose and juggle three balls with each hand. He walked around backward, then caught the balls and slipped them into the huge pockets of the baggy patched suit he wore for his act.

"I guess nobody would let Rajah get at him unless he was crazy," I answered. "Did anybody ever find out how Rajah got in?"

"Nobody's saying, but it's not too hard to figure."

Just then the band began playing the march that

was his cue. Before he ducked out the door, he stopped and looked at me with a serious look on his painted face. "Who can you think of who *wasn't* inside at the celebration, who handles cats all the time, who doesn't like you, and has been in the vicinity of every 'accident' we've had?"

"You have to mean Rex. But how are we going to prove it, Felipe?"

"Somebody's gonna have to watch him all the time," he said. "Maybe you can do some of that—with your brothers." He ducked out and headed for the Big Top, and I knew what I wanted to do.

When we first came to work, we went to every performance, but I guess even a circus gets to be routine. Now while I was waiting for the Flying Cortinas to do their stuff and use me to help with the rigging, I wandered around and talked to people.

Joe and Jake were over at the sideshow tent, where they usually were. When I first started going there, it made me nervous. I didn't know how to talk to those "unusual people." But pretty soon I found out they were just like anyone else.

Jake was talking to Lou, who was in his clown costume and ready to go on. He was showing Jake how to swallow a sword. Lou had done just about everything in the way of circus acts—fire-eater, acrobat, clown, bareback rider. He'd taken the yo-yo invention and was really making it the highlight of the circus. And he always gave the credit to Joe, too.

"Ah, Lou," Jake said with a grin, "I know that trick. The sword folds up into the handle! You don't think I'm a rube, do you?"

Lou laughed and held the sword up. It was about eighteen inches long and had a heavy-looking hilt. "You say the blade goes up into this?" Lou asked, pointing at the hilt.

"Sure it does, Lou!" Jake gave me a wink. "Nobody could shove a *real* sword down his throat."

"Look here, then." Lou grinned, removing the heavy hilt of the sword. There was nothing but a blade with a bare spot where the hilt had come off. Lou winked at me, tilted his head back, and raised the blade. He let the thing slide down his throat until his fingers touched his lips, then pulled it out.

"How about that, Jake?" He laughed, then reached into a box beside the wall and pulled out what looked like a long neon tube. He plugged one end of an electric cord into the wall and pulled his shirt off, exposing a hairy chest thick as a keg. He flipped a switch that was on one end of the thing, and it lit up with a green glow. "Now, you Buck boys, watch this trick!"

It was sort of scary when he put the tube into his mouth and let it slide down his throat. We could see the green light going right down so that he had a line of green showing through his body down to his belt!

Jake gulped, and so did I. When Lou pulled it out and laughed, I said, "What if that tube broke inside your throat, Lou?"

"I make sure that doesn't happen, Barney, but it could." He began packing up the tube and added, "It can always happen to any of us. Look at Felipe."

"What about Felipe?" Jake asked.

"You haven't heard about that?" Lou slipped back into his shirt. "The Flying Cortinas once included Thomas, Lillian, and Felipe—best act in the circus world. They were so good nobody else was even mentioned in the same breath with them. Everybody said Felipe was as good as Cordona!"

"Why did he decide to quit?"

Lou made a face. "He didn't *decide*—he fell. Coming out of a triple, he missed the hands of Thomas by one inch, and that was it!"

"I bet Mr. Cortina felt bad," I said.

"Everybody did. Thomas the most, even though it wasn't his fault. And Lillian, too. She'd married Thomas only about a month before the fall, but for a long time nobody knew if she'd marry Thomas or Felipe. They both courted her, you know."

"But, Lou, he doesn't seem hurt," I said.

"Oh, not *bad,* Barney, but it hurt his back and he

never recovered his timing. Those fellows are so finely tuned, just one hairbreadth off is all it takes. But Felipe has made it. He's a good clown—and that's not as easy as most people think."

"Who's the best clown in the circus, Lou?" Jake asked.

"Me! No contest!" He grinned. "And when I get the Magic Yo-Yo perfected, it'll be known to the entire world that Lou is *the* man!"

He ran off to do his act, and I told Jake about what Felipe had said about Rex Rogers. "We gotta watch that cat, Jake! Now what I want to do is sort of divide up— you, me, and Joe. We'll all take turns watching him. Like I'll watch him in the mornings, you and Joe take the rest of the day, and we'll work out something about nights."

"Hey, I'll bet we can get a picture of him trying to do something and laying it on the Phantom! Joe's fixed that camera he brought, and we can take turns carrying it. Get the real evidence on that joker. Say, I bet Mr. Cortina will give us a reward!"

I shook my head sadly. "You never give up looking for a profit, do you, Jake?"

Jake acted hurt. "I'm doing it to help him out. If Mr. Cortina wants to give me a reward, what am I supposed to do? Turn him down?"

There was no arguing with Jake. That much was obvious.

We decided that we'd split up the duty so that someone was keeping an eye on Rex Rogers almost around the clock. I don't think he ever caught on, because Jake is a natural-born sneak and Joe isn't really noticeable anyway. Once Rogers nearly ran over me as he came out of the cook tent, and he gave me a hard look. "You always seem to be in the way, kid. Stay clear of me, and stay away from my daughter!"

Later that afternoon, Jake said, "We'll get him, Barney. Don't you worry. He's got to make a move pretty soon, and we'll nail him with evidence!"

But we didn't!

We pulled the tents down the next day and were just ready to start out for our next location when it happened. One of the big diesel trucks had been running, then coughed and quit. The driver worked on it for an hour, but it wouldn't start. Then another truck quit, and it acted just the same way. Almost in the space of five minutes, two more trucks stopped dead.

Suddenly Marty Ramos, the boss canvas man, started shouting, "Shut down the engines!" as loudly as he could. Then Marty and a couple of the men started pulling apart the engine of the first truck that had quit.

We were all standing around watching when Marty came out from under the hood and said to Mr. Cortina, "Bad news, Thomas. These engines are ruined!"

"*All* of them?" Mr. Cortina asked, his face in shock. "What's the matter, Marty?"

Marty looked around and finally met the eyes of the owner. "I'd have to say the Phantom has struck again, and this time he's done a good job. There's sugar in all these gas tanks. At least, there is in this one, and I'd guess that's what's wrong with the others."

"Sugar in the gas tank!" Mr. Cortina gasped. "But what does that do?"

"The sugar melts and gets into the whole system. Then it turns to a sort of gum and freezes up the engine."

"Can't . . . can't they be fixed?" he asked in a small voice.

"These'll all have to have their engines completely overhauled. The rest'll have to have their gas tanks pulled and changed. I'd guess most of them are in the same shape. Don't let anyone start a single engine until we find out if there's sugar in the tank."

"But we have to be in Shreveport tonight!" he protested.

"Not with these trucks, Thomas," Marty said with a shrug. "It'll take at least a week and a pile of money. You know how much those diesel shops charge."

Mr. Cortina turned pale. "See how many will have to be repaired, Marty. I'll go try to find the money."

Everybody was babbling and wandering around, and I got to Jake as quickly as I could. "Did you see Rogers go near the trucks after you relieved me?"

"No, I . . . well, I . . ."

I grabbed him. "Jake, you *did* watch him, didn't you?"

"Well, sure I did, Barney, except for just about half an hour!" He saw I was getting upset, so he went on. "But he was asleep, Barney. He couldn't have done it!"

"How do you *know* he was asleep if you weren't there to watch him?"

"I know because Dee Dee told me so!" he snapped back. "She came out and I just casually asked her where her dad was and that's what she said."

"And what was to keep him from getting up, you turkey? And where did you have to go that was so important?"

"Well, I wasn't going to tell you until we got done." Jake squirmed. "But me and Joe have practically finished our next invention, and when we get—"

"I don't want to hear it, Jake!" I said, slapping my hands over my ears. "You're *not* getting me involved, do you hear?"

He began to babble about how great it was and how it couldn't miss, but that was an old song to me!

The circus equipment was all packed and ready to go, but I couldn't think of any way we were going to be in Shreveport by night. Mr. Cortina managed it somehow. He hired some trucks to hook up to the semitrailers, and we all piled in and left. We had to leave some people behind to drive the vehicles after they were checked out. By the time we got set up, all of the trucks that hadn't gone to the shop for overhauls were pulled up close to the Big Top.

We were all falling-down tired, but that evening after the show, I went on over to the Cortinas' tent to give Angel her lessons as usual. Jake went with me, leaving Joe to watch Rogers.

It wasn't much fun. Lou was doing a lot of bookkeeping and accounting for Mr. Cortina. They kept going over a stack of paper a mile high. Mrs. Cortina talked to Jake, telling him about when she was a girl, and I tried to explain *Silas Marner* to Angel, who really didn't want to understand it.

Finally Mr. Cortina threw a pencil against the wall. "We can't do it! There is no possible way to make enough to keep this circus. No way on earth!"

Mrs. Cortina and Angel looked at each other, sadness clouding both their faces. "You may be right this time," Lou said with a wave of his hand at the papers. "No matter how we add them up, if we don't have fifty thousand dollars in less than two months, Milo Hunter wins."

Mr. Cortina put his head over his fists on the table. "I've tried so hard! God knows I've given it everything I have, and still it's not enough!"

I gulped and added my two cents' worth. "God won't let you down, Mr. Cortina."

He tried to smile and nodded. "I wish I could think so, Barney, but if God doesn't help us, we can't go on."

"Mr. Cortina, I know how you can do it!"

Jake Buck got up and walked right over to where he was sitting. I gaped at Jake and almost told him to shut up, but he spoke before I could. "You ever hear of the Super Bowl, Mr. Cortina?"

Mr. Cortina was a real sports fan and grinned a little. "Sure, everybody knows the Super Bowl."

"It's when the two best teams get together at the end of the season to play the Big Game. And everybody watches it, right?"

"Sure, but what's that got to do with us?"

"Why, it's simple." Jake spread his hands out and looked at us as if we were pretty dumb not to have thought of it. "Why not have a Super Circus at the end of the season?"

"A Super Circus?" he asked, bewildered. I saw a sudden gleam in Lou's eyes.

"Sure!" Jake went on with sudden excitement. "What you do is get all the circuses to agree to come to one place with their best acts at the end of the season, see? And you get a huge crowd there to see the winners of the contests. All we have to do to get all the money is win!"

"That's an idea, boss," Lou said suddenly. "It might work!"

"But who'd put up the money?" Mr. Cortina asked.

Lou jumped up and began to wave his arms around. "You got to think *big,* Thomas. Like you got to think about Madison Square Garden! You got to think about all the publicity we'd get! Why, we could offer a fifty-thousand-dollar prize for the best flying act and prizes for the best clown act. I'd be a cinch to win *that* one with the Magic Yo-Yo! Why, it can't miss!" He looked at Jake with admiration and shook his head. "Kid, you're going to own the United States when you get grown!"

"But would the other circuses go for it, Lou?" Mr. Cortina asked, obviously getting excited now.

"Why, sure they would! Because we wouldn't have to take the whole show, just the acts we want in the competition!" Suddenly Mr. Cortina jumped up and grabbed his wife up so easily you'd have thought she weighed ten ounces. He began to shout, and we all went sort of crazy, jumping around. I was hanging on to Angel and she was hanging on to me and Lou had flipped Jake upside down and was shaking him like a trip-hammer!

Finally we settled down, and Mr. Cortina said, "This is going to work, but we have to have the very best acts. We must get this idea going and win if we're going to keep our circus out of Milo Hunter's hands."

"The Magic Yo-Yo is a shoo-in," Lou said. "It's new, and that's always two-thirds of the way home with a clown act. We need a few new wrinkles on the Flying

Cortinas, and you ought to win the trapeze act. We need one more winner."

"I've got it," Jake said, stepping up with the look on his face that had always meant trouble for me.

"You're going to do a high-wire act, Jake?" Lou laughed. Everybody knew Jake wasn't going to get any higher off the ground than stepping up on the curb.

Jake didn't laugh. "Now, let's get one thing straight. The *last* time we came up with a great idea—the Human Yo-Yo—you wouldn't let us do it."

"Now, Jake, that was too dangerous." Mrs. Cortina said.

Jake grinned. "That's all right, but this time before I tell you about the act that's going to win the grand prize for new acts, you gotta promise that nobody but the *Bucks* get to do the act!"

"Now, I *cannot* promise that," Mr. Cortina began to argue, but Jake didn't budge. For over an hour they tried to get him to compromise, but he had that hard look on his face, and I knew they were wasting their time. When my brother Jake got an idea, he held onto it until it thundered!

This time Jake knew he had them. "You need this act to win enough money to keep the Cortina Brothers' Circus on the road, Mr. Cortina. Now, yes or no?"

"Yes," Mr. Cortina finally said, despite warning looks from his wife and Angel. "All right, Jake, what's this new act of yours?"

Jake grinned like a shark who'd just gotten a fine new meal to bite into. "Call it 'Barney Buck—the Human Slingshot'! How do you like that, brother?" he said to me. "You're going to be a *star!*"

"No, I'm probably going to be in great pain and mental anguish over all this. . . ."

Angel started to protest, so I held up my hand. "Never mind, Angel, it goes with being the brother of Jake Buck, the eighth wonder of the world when it comes to nutty schemes!"

8

The Human Slingshot

MR. Cortina stopped me the next day as I was coming out of the cook tent. "Well, Barney, your Super Circus idea went over."

"Hey, that's great!"

"Milo Hunter will be the promoter," he said with a frown. "He'll make a mint, like he always does. And he'll expect us to lose so he can get my outfit."

"But, Mr. Cortina," I said anxiously, "won't he pick the judges and things like that?"

"No! They will be chosen by the circus performers themselves. I saw to that! We will have a fair chance, but that is all. Now we must work hard and be ready to compete with the finest performers in the world. I have already started to work with Juan on the triple, and we will win! Nobody else can do that trick so well. By the way, how are you doing with your act?"

I wished he hadn't asked! "Well, I'm *thinking* about it . . . ," I managed to say.

"No! Either you must do it, or get someone else," he said, putting his hand on my shoulder. "And to be honest, I wish you would get somebody else—a real acrobat! It is too dangerous for you, Barney. You could get hurt."

I thought so, too, and I was just about ready to say so. "I'll let you know, Mr. Cortina. Tomorrow at the latest."

Jake and Joe had come up with a lulu this time. After our meeting at the Cortinas', when Jake had come up with the Super Circus idea, I told them to show me that fool slingshot the next morning.

Right after breakfast we went behind the trailer area, where Joe had a big drawing board. We sat down, and Joe pulled the board out of the canvas cover and showed me this picture:

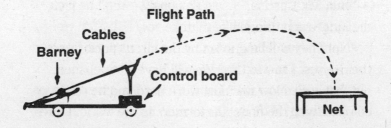

"See, Barney," he said, pointing with his pencil. "It's just like the catapult we had back on the Caddo River, only bigger."

I remembered *that* all right! Joe and Jake had rigged up a device with cables made of surgical rubber tubing. It had been a huge slingshot attached to a sled. Somebody would get on the sled, and when the thing went off, it would shoot him right out over a bluff so that he'd go high into the air and fall into the river below. It worked, and it was fun, too. The only reason we quit was because a little kid broke his arm doing it.

"See, you just lie down on your stomach, and this slingshot lets go. It shoots you in this curve way up high, and you fall into the net. It won't be hard, Barney."

I stared at the drawing. "How *high* into the air will I go?"

"Oh, you ought to go up about eighty or ninety feet," Jake said coolly. "It wouldn't be any good if you went only ten feet or twenty. What we do is shoot you *way* up—close to the top of the tent, see?"

"And you want your own brother to do *that?*" I asked. "I could kill myself!"

"Gimme a break, Barney!" Jake snorted. "You've been practicing falling into that net all summer. I've seen you! It's just a matter of timing."

"Easy for you to say," I said. "You don't have to get on this fool thing! Why do *I* have to do it?"

"Because you have to help Mr. Cortina save his circus, Barney," Joe said. He looked so earnest. . . . I could never look at him without thinking of Mom. He looked exactly like her, and he was about all I had left of her. Jake looked like Dad with his dark hair. I don't know who I looked like with my red hair and freckles. Dad used to say he found me under a mulberry bush!

But even to please Joe, I was leery of doing the Slingshot. I'd enjoyed the catapult on the river, but this was different. A guy could get hurt!

"I think we ought to let Juan or some other acrobat do it," I said.

That took real character on my part, because Juan had never let up on me. But I knew I wasn't all that noble. I was just trying to get out of doing the Slingshot!

Actually it was Juan who made up my mind to do the act.

Later that afternoon, I was checking the rigging in the top and had decided to ask Juan to do the Slingshot. He and Angel were working on their act. I checked all the lines, and when they were finished, Juan was on the platform with me. Angel was on the other platform forty feet away.

I had opened my mouth to ask Juan if he'd like to do the act, when he pushed me off the platform. He didn't put his hands out and shove me off. Nothing that obvious. He just brushed against me, and since I was standing on the edge and not holding onto anything, I just fell off from the pressure he'd put on me.

The net was there, but I knew that I'd hit the edge. Doing that was just about as bad as hitting the ground! It could've smashed my spine like a rotten twig.

When I saw the ground rushing up like a wall, I screamed. Then I hit. I managed to roll over as I fell and hit the net on my back and shoulders. I bounced up, and instead of being thrown out toward the ground, I bounced *in* toward the center of the net! That was why I didn't get killed.

When I looked up, Juan's dark face was peering down. "What you squealing about, rube?" he said in a mocking voice. "You sound like a pig getting his throat cut! You some kind of girl to scream like that?"

"Barney!" Angel flew down the ladder and came to me like a bird. "Are you all right?" She caught me around the neck as I stopped bouncing, and I wish she hadn't!

"Sure, the putz is all right, Angel. He's just a little bird that fell off his perch!" Juan grinned. "You heard him scream, Angel? Sounded like an old maid who found a burglar under her bed, didn't he?"

"Are you all right?" she asked again, her dark eyes filled with concern.

"Sure," I muttered—but all I could think was, *I screamed!* I felt humiliated.

That did it, I guess. I climbed down off the net and went straight to where Jake and Joe were putting the finishing touches on the Slingshot.

"I'm ready, you guys," I said with such force they stared at me. "Well, let's get on with the program!"

"Sure, Barney," Joe said. "We're ready, if you're sure you want to do it."

"It's just another catapult," I said. "Let's go."

They kept staring at me. Then Jake said, "It'll be a piece of cake!"

I crawled up into the thing, and there was a place for my feet to fit. "Put your hands out straight, Barney," Joe directed, "and keep your legs braced. That's where the force will be. Then when we touch the trigger, you'll go off just like in the catapult."

"But you have to turn a somersault and land on your back," Jake said.

"I know that!" I snapped. "Let's just begin with a short one, all right?"

"Sure!" Joe grinned. "See, we've got this board set so we can send you ten feet or a hundred feet."

"What's to keep me from going too straight?" I asked.

"Oh, I've got that all figured out," Joe said, pointing to a series of dials on the board before him. "This sets the curve to fit the pressure. If I set it for ten feet, it'll be a real short arc, so the platform is almost flat. See?" I saw the platform lower until it was almost level with the ground. "But if you're going fifty feet, the platform lifts, and that lets you sort of *curve,* and you go a long way." He touched the board, and I saw the platform elevate and the rubber cable tighten.

"What's your master plan, Jake?" I asked. "You going to shoot me to the moon eventually?"

"No," he said seriously. "The most is about a hundred feet. That'll make you fly off in a nice curve. To the customers it'll look like Superman flying to rescue Lois Lane. You ready?"

"I guess so." I climbed into the sled and steadied my feet on a wooden block. "How far am I going this time?"

"Only ten feet or so," Joe said. "Here goes. One . . . two . . . three!"

He slapped at the board, and I felt the pressure on my feet as the rubber cables caught. It was just like the time with the catapult, and it was really fun!

I was conscious of a blur as I was thrown into the air, but I'd learned how to keep my body straight as I left the sled. It was no trick to let myself slowly turn in a slow somersault. I did a perfect hit with my back and shoulders into the net and sprang up easily, making a little bow like an acrobat.

"Great!" Jake shouted. "You looked great!"

Joe grinned from ear to ear, and I felt pretty good!

"Let's try for about twenty feet," I said. Joe fiddled with the settings, and this time I was off a little, landing on my feet and getting tossed by the net. But the next time I allowed for the distance and made a perfect landing.

We messed with the thing all afternoon. After awhile I noticed that Mr. Cortina and Angel, along with quite a few of the performers, had gathered to watch.

"Let's try a hard one, Joe," I said. "How about fifty feet?"

He set the controls, and I got on. This time I made the biggest arc ever, but I made the turn, landed just right, and sprang up with one bound. I turned to the performers and said, "Ta-daaaaa!" with a big bow.

They all applauded, and Mr. Cortina cried out, "Bravo! Bravo!"

It was pretty nice, you know? They made a big fuss over me, and all of them told me it was going to be a great act and that I was a born performer and all that kind of stuff.

Even Dee Dee had managed to stand close. She hung onto my arm with her blue eyes sparkling. "You were wonderful, Barney! Just wonderful!"

I got a glimpse of Juan, who had a look on his face that would have soured milk. But he patted me on the shoulder and said, "Very *good,* my friend!" I knew it nearly broke his heart to say it!

Angel gave me a nice smile, and Lou patted me as high on the back as he could reach—about belt high!

That evening during our time together in the trailer, Mr. Cortina interrupted Angel and me to say, "Barney, how'd you like to be a local hero?"

"What do you mean?" I asked.

He gave me a grin and waved a sheet of paper under my nose. "We'll be in Pine Bluff, Arkansas, in two weeks. That's close to your hometown, isn't it?"

"Sure is!"

"Well, what I'm thinking is that if you can get your act together by then, we could really clean up!"

"How?"

"Why, all we have to do is let the fact be known that a local son is the *star* of the circus."

"But I'm no star!"

"You will be by then, at least on paper!" He laughed. "All we have to do is have the publicity stress the 'death-defying Barney Buck—the Human Slingshot'!"

"Shoot, it's not *that* dangerous!" I said.

"No, but it will be on the posters," he said with a smile. Then he got serious. "But it *is* dangerous, Barney. I don't want you to forget that. If you were off one half-turn in your somersault, or if the Slingshot itself were off by a few degrees, you could be shot into the stands and kill some spectators—not to mention yourself. So you must always check and check again! You understand?"

"Sure, but we always do that. Joe never moves away from the controls."

"Good! But never stop checking. That is the secret of every performer!"

He then left with his wife to see some other performers.

"You'll be the *star,* Barney!" Angel said, leaning on me and looking up at me with those big, dark eyes. Her breath smelled really sweet. She was just a kid, and I intended to talk to her about leaning on guys, but to tell the truth, I really didn't mind having her look at me like that. So I just tried to be cool.

"Oh, it's no big deal, Angel."

"It is so!" she said and leaned on me again. "That girl who came to see you—what was her name?"

"Oh, you mean Debra?"

"I guess." She reached up and touched my forehead. "What made that scar?"

"Jake hit me with a stick."

"Oh. Do you and Debra go together?"

"No! I mean, we're good friends, just real good buddies, you know?"

She stared at me. "Are we good friends, Barney?"

"Why, sure we are."

"*Real* good friends, Barney?" she whispered. Then she pulled her lips close to my ear. "Are we better friends than you and Debra? Are we?"

Whatever I said at that point didn't make much sense. I think I said that we were *more* than good friends, and then she gave me a squeeze and said, "Good! Now you can tell Debra I'm your girl, can't you, Barney?"

I don't think I actually said that, but she seemed to think so. Anyway, how was I going to tell Debra all that?

I had only one thought: *Maybe the Slingshot'll shoot me into the menagerie tent, and I won't have to worry about Debra and Angel and Dee Dee and all that stuff.*

Somehow I knew I wouldn't be so lucky!

9

The Circus Goes to Church

WELL, I say we make it look as much like a real slingshot as we can!"

"No, Lou, what we need is to cover up the cables and stuff!"

Jake was trying to run everybody's business as usual, but he'd run head-on into Lou Beauchamp. The clown, just as stubborn as Jake, bobbed his head from side to side and poked Jake with a stubby forefinger to explain his point. We'd been putting the finishing touches on the Slingshot, but Jake wanted to disguise it.

"Look, kid," Lou said, "Hugo Zacchini did a human cannonball act back in 1929—and he just copied what a girl named Rose Richter did when the Barnum-Bailey was just startin'. Zacchini had a great big cannon that used compressed air and shot him up seventy feet high. Made it look like a real cannon—with smoke and noise."

"That's what *we* gotta do!" Jake argued.

"Nope, it's been done, kid. This one ain't. We got a new thing, and that's what makes the circus go." He waved his hand at the Slingshot. "We gotta make it look just like a slingshot as much as we can. Everybody's used one. We build up tension by starting in slow, and we let the crowd see that cable stretched back sooo hard! Then harder and harder! By the time we pull it all the way back, why, they'll be holding their breath!"

Lou was right, as usual. He always was about the circus. We made a fancy carriage for the Slingshot, with the cables attached to the sled that I hung on to. We made the uprights higher, and the form actually looked like a slingshot.

"What makes it accurate?" Mr. Cortina asked, staring at it, not at all satisfied. "Just one shot too far and you're in trouble."

Joe piped up from where he was sitting by the control panel, "Look here, Mr. Cortina." He put his hand on a dial that had numbers and pointed to a control that allowed the Slingshot to be pulled to a given slot. "See those numbers? Well, they change the tension on the cable. And here's a control for the weight of the performer. And when you line those two up, why you can look right at this scale and see two things: how high he'll go and how far he'll go. So all you have to do is set the Slingshot right, and it'll put Barney right on target."

A little mutter of appreciation went around the crowd that had gathered to watch, and Joe blushed. "You did good, Joe," Lou said. "Now, you folks move back and let the world's greatest slingshot artist get to his practice."

I climbed up on the sled, and Joe asked, "How about if I take you about ten feet higher, Barney?"

"Let 'er go, Joe!" I shouted. I braced my feet and grasped the handholds designed to give me better balance. Then I felt a tremble in the machine. Suddenly everything blurred from the fast takeoff, and all the blood seemed to run to my feet. I felt my body leave the sled. It was *fun* arcing up and over. It was like flying! I'd done it enough so that making the drop (that is, rolling over so that I hit on my back) was a piece of cake!

A round of applause went up as I hit the net, bounded up, and took a fancy bow the way circus people do. Then Lou said, "Good enough, Barney, but you can save the bows until you've made the big jump."

By that he meant having the Slingshot at full power, enough to make me go over 150 feet in the air. It didn't look possible, but with steady practice and by adding a few feet more each day, by the end of the week I did it!

Everybody was there to catch it, and I guess I was feeling pretty proud. Not bad for a Goober Holler rube!

There were only a couple of sour notes. Juan sneered and turned away saying, "He moves like a fat turkey!" Rex Rogers just laughed and said in that hateful way of his, "Maybe if you're lucky, Thomas, he'll miss the net! Then he won't be an embarrassment to the show."

Mr. Cortina stared at him. "You take care of your own act, Rex. Barney, he's going to be a real trouper!"

Rex went off all huffy, and it had done me good to see Mr. Cortina put him down. The trouble was that I liked Dee Dee. She was a really good kid. I'd been careful not to say much to her since her dad had made it clear he didn't want us to be friends. But several times Dee Dee had begged me to help her with her English, and we'd met late when Rex was out doing something. "I don't like to sneak around, Dee Dee," I told her once.

"Me either, but I get so lonesome. Daddy doesn't have any friends, and I guess he doesn't want me to have any. If it weren't for Ruth, I'd go crazy."

Ruth Stratton was one of the high-wire performers and seemed to put up with Rex Rogers better than anyone else. Maybe she liked him, but I didn't see how.

Anyway, before I knew it, Mr. Cortina was clapping his hand on my shoulder and saying, "Tomorrow night, Barney! That'll be your big night!"

"Yeah, but I gotta tell you I'm pretty nervous, Mr. Cortina."

We were pulling the rigging down and getting ready

to move to Pine Bluff, Arkansas, only about forty miles from Goober Holler.

"You *should* be nervous," he said with a smile. "You'd be a bad performer if you weren't. But when you climb on the sled tomorrow night, why, you'll have nerves of steel, Barney! Did I tell you the performance is sold out? Sure! I had a story put in the *Arkansas Gazette* and all the local papers in the little towns. I can see the headlines now: 'Local Boy Daredevil Comes Home!' Oh, it'll be the best town we've had this summer!"

He was right about that. When I came out at the beginning of the Spec (the big parade), I couldn't see an empty seat. I gulped and looked around to see if anyone from Goober Holler was actually there, but it wasn't hard to find them.

Across from the center ring was a big cloth sign that said, WELCOME HOME, BARNEY! Right there. In a special section. I could see Coach and Uncle Dave and all the Simmons family and Chief Tanner and the whole Boys' Club—just about everybody!

That made me want to run and hide. It was one thing to practice the Big Jump when it was nice and quiet with just circus people around, but here with all the noise and the band blaring and the smell of popcorn and hot dogs and animals and people—well, that was something else!

I can't remember much about the show, but I must

have gotten into my costume somehow. I wore blue tights with a white cape all studded with red stars. It really made me look like a wimp—tall and gangly as I was. Angel said I looked fine, but Juan said I looked like a flagpole decked out for the Fourth of July.

I must have just gone into a funk, because when I heard the music that was my cue, I just clung to a tent pole in my dressing room and wouldn't budge. I was standing there like a rock when Angel came in. I guess she saw I was frozen, because she came up and gave me that big smile of hers and patted me on the shoulder.

"Sure, I know, Barney. You think all of us haven't been like that? But you're a real kinker now, and I know you're not going to let us down. Come on. Your friends are waiting to see you." She sort of talked me away from that pole, and I found myself walking out into the center of the Big Top.

There was a roll of drums, and the ringmaster bellowed out, "And now, the most daring, death-defying act on the continent—the Human Slingshot—will hurl the daring Barney Buck 175 feet through the air at a speed of over one hundred miles per hour. He'll land in the net, but one false move and the daring young man will be killed instantly!"

He stretched the truth like always, but even *I* got to believing it. Now, with the drums rolling and the music building up, I felt just like a robot!

I climbed into the sled and nodded at Joe, who sent me off on the short jump. I got through it. The hollering and applause amazed me. I felt pretty good when I went back and took the Big Jump. I did it just right, arcing up high, close to the canvas, then making my turn and falling into the net. It was like taking a jump shot in basketball. In the whole world of the circus, those jumps were *all* I could do.

But I was a hit! The whole crowd roared and cheered, and I had to keep on making those crazy bows and waving my hands around the way Lou told me to. For a transplanted Yankee trying to make it through algebra class in Goober Holler, Arkansas, those cheers were sweet to my ears!

Coach, Uncle Dave, Debra, and a bunch of other people came to my dressing room and congratulated me. It was pretty crowded in the tent, but nobody seemed to care.

Everybody was trying to talk at once, and finally Coach got the floor. "Barney, I want to invite you and the whole circus to church Sunday morning. It'll be your day at our church. What do you say?"

I didn't have to answer, because Mr. Cortina had just come in to shake hands with them all. "We'll be there, Coach!" he boomed out. "Tell that preacher to have a good sermon, all right?"

Except for a few men to keep watch, *everybody* went

that Sunday! A few tried to argue, but Mr. Cortina assigned Heck Rawlings and Lou Beauchamp to deal with them.

Lou just motioned to Heck and said, "Take 'em in, Heck—dressed or undressed!" One look at Heck's bulging muscles and not a single performer said no.

We'd had a few revivals at our church when every seat was packed, but nothing like this. Coach must've gotten to Brother Jenkins, the pastor, because when we pulled in and went inside, it looked like a circus.

For one thing, the pulpit was gone. Instead there was a ring with a little stand in the middle for the preacher to speak from. Overhead was a trapeze. The ushers were dressed like clowns. My church had gone all out to make the people from the Cortina Brothers' Circus feel at home! Usually when we went to church with the Cortinas, people either were too polite or else they didn't even look at us. This service was aimed right at them.

I think it worked. I saw the Living Skeleton look around and mutter to the Fattest Woman in the World, "Hey, this is nice, Emma, you know?"

When Brother Jenkins got up to preach, he didn't mess around. But then he never did!

"Ye must be born again!" he said, then read from the Bible about how Nicodemus had gone to Jesus by night and Jesus had told him he had to be saved. Brother

Jenkins wasn't a shouting type of preacher, but looking into his eyes was like looking down a gun barrel!

He preached a simple sermon about Jesus' dying for circus people, just like he had died for regular people. Brother Jenkins kept using the language of the circus. He said that angels were like web-sitters, watching out for the performers and seeing they didn't fall! I guess it came as a shock to Mr. Cortina to learn that he had an angel assigned to him personally!

Circus people call the trip from the place to where the last show is given back to the circus headquarters the *Home Run.* At the end of the sermon Brother Jenkins said:

"Sooner or later, you'll have to think of the last Home Run. Then all the applause will cease. The band will fall silent. The rigging will all come down, and every kinker will take off his costume for the last time. The razor-backs will pull the Big Top down for the last time. It'll be Home Sweet Home."

I was surprised he knew that term, *Home Sweet Home,* which is what the circus folks called the last show of the season.

Brother Jenkins went on. "I want to ask all of you who are here—when you take off your paint for the last time, turn your last triple, hear the last call for doors, what then? What will you do for all eternity?"

Then he closed with, "If you would like to put your

Home Sweet Home in the hands of a man called Jesus, I can't think of a better time to do it."

Some of them did! One of the riggers, an animal handler who worked for Rex Rogers, and a little old lady who'd been a trapeze artist and now helped with the costumes went forward and committed themselves to Jesus Christ! Lots of others seemed to be thinking about it but were too embarrassed to go—Angel, for one.

After church there was a fellowship dinner for all who wanted to stay. The church women had brought a lot of food, and we had a fantastic meal. All the circus performers and the church members were mixing around, and I thought it was fine!

Coach Littlejohn thought so, too, because he gave me a big hug after I'd downed so much pie and cake I felt almost helpless. "I think you did real fine, Barney, bringing these folks here!" He grinned.

I knew he was excited about seeing people get right with God, and I sure was happy to see him proud of me.

Later I found Debra and Coach and some of the others just sitting around drinking coffee and lemonade. Then suddenly Angel asked Coach, "Does being a Christian mean you have to love *everybody?*"

I was trying to ignore Angel and pay attention to Debra, but Angel had spoken so sharply that everybody sort of looked up. She had a puzzled look on her face.

114

"Well, I guess you're right, Angel," Coach said. He grinned that Robert Redford–type grin at her.

But even though Angel appreciated his good looks, she said, "Nobody can do that, Mr. Littlejohn! I mean, what if they're awful?"

She shot me a quick glance. All of a sudden I felt sick because I knew where she was headed!

"Suppose someone is just terrible, would you have to love him anyway?" she asked, looking right at me. "We have a man named Rex Rogers, and he's not nice at all. Would a Christian have to love *him?*"

Every head turned to stare at me. If I had ever been on the spot in my life, this was it! They knew I didn't like Rex Rogers, and they waited to see what Coach would say.

Coach was smart. "I'd have to say, if a fellow is a Christian, he can't pick and choose who his favorites will be. Jesus didn't!"

"But how can you make yourself love somebody who's been mean to you?"

Coach looked at Angel, then answered, "You can't, not as a natural reaction. If somebody slaps you on the cheek, the world says to give them a shot! But Jesus said to turn the other cheek."

I looked around. Just about everybody—Lou, Mr. and Mrs. Cortina, Angel, Juan, Felipe—was frozen, waiting for Coach to go on.

The Coach smiled and shrugged his shoulders. "If a person gives his life to Jesus of Nazareth, he writes a blank check, telling God to fill it in. As a Christian I don't have any choice but to love the person who crosses my path. That's what God does. He loves us all."

I felt small enough to walk under the *door!* I'd been mouthing off about what a rotten guy Rex Rogers was and claiming to be a Christian! I began getting strange looks from the circus people, so I quickly excused myself and walked out.

It's funny how easy being a Christian seems when you read about it, but how hard it is to be one in the real world!

10

Taking a Backseat

WE stayed at Pine Bluff for four days. Since I was so close to home, I decided to go to Goober Holler, pick up Tim, and head for the woods. I was all practiced up, and Mr. Cortina said it would do me good to take a break. I ended up taking Angel and Juan along with me.

I hadn't planned to, but Angel had begged me. "I want to see your home, Barney," she'd said. When she waved those eyelashes at me and pouted with those cherry-red lips of hers, what could I do?

"I guess I'll go, too!" Juan had said with a crooked grin. He'd been listening to Angel, and he never wanted to let us have a minute together.

I knew he just wanted to spoil the day, but all of a

sudden I had an idea. I grinned at him and said, "Sure, Juan, be glad to have you!"

He got a little suspicious, but he wasn't about to let Angel run off with me alone. When we were ready to go, he was our chauffeur. We piled into one of the pickups and made our way over Highway 270 to Goober Holler, stopping only to pick up Tim, my black-and-tan hound, from Chief Tanner.

"He's ready for a run, Barney," Chief Tanner said with a grin. "He's been run pretty often since you been gone. And I tell you, there ain't no better dog that I know of!"

We put Tim in the truck bed and went to my house. I showed Juan and Angel around the place. It wasn't much—just an old farmhouse with a garden behind, lots of big oak trees shading the roof, and a pond packed with bluegills and young bass to the south. Juan gave it a quick look and said, "Boy! I'd hate to be stuck *here!*"

Angel had a warm light in her dark eyes as she looked around, then said, "It's real nice, Barney. I like it!"

We had just a few hours, but I was anxious to see if Tim still knew his stuff. A good coon dog wasn't hard to find around Goober Holler, but I had big things in mind for Tim. I knew he had it in him to be a national champion! And if I had my way, that was what he'd be!

Finally, we were off. It was great to be in the woods again, listening to the coyotes bawling and the hawks screaming when they'd lost a mouse in the stubble of the cornfield! Just smelling the woods and the fallow ground—and watching a pair of white-tailed deer go bounding and floating over the rise and over an old fence—were enough to make me want to quit the circus and come home!

I guess I forgot about Juan and Angel. It was easy for me to follow Tim through the thickets and the briers because I was used to it. But after about an hour I realized they'd gotten lost or left behind. I whistled Tim back from the hot trail of a boar coon and backtracked until I found them.

They were a sight!

Both of them were scratched from the saw briers and flushed from trying to keep up with me. I felt sorry for Angel, but it sort of gave me a kick to see Juan trapped in a ravine, scared to death of snakes, and looking lost as a goose!

"You look like you need a hand, Juan," I called out. He looked helpless—the way I'd looked for so long. He'd always been in control up there on the high trapeze!

"Get me . . . out of this place!" he gasped.

"I guess we all have our place, don't we, Juan?" I said, leading him out of the patch of briers and clinging vines that grabbed at him. "You sure look better up on the bar than you do here!"

He glared at me, and I couldn't resist saying, "Guess

you're not ever going to make a good hunter, Juan. Better stick to the trapeze!"

I held Angel's hand and led her back to the house with Juan close behind. Suddenly I thought about what Coach had said about loving your enemies, so I turned and said, "Hey, Juan, I know it's rough for a guy who's never been there to go through the woods. You want to take a break?"

"Just get me *out* of this place!" he said, barely above a whisper. Angel giggled and pressed my hand. We made it back to the pickup and dropped Tim off at Chief Tanner's for safekeeping.

Back at the circus, Juan disappeared without a backward look. Angel smiled and said, "Thanks for showing me your home, Barney. It was fun!"

I thought I'd gotten Juan pretty well into a corner, but he was smarter than I thought. The next day he came over while I was practicing. The scratches on his face were still pretty bad. He didn't say much at first.

Mr. Cortina and Lou were leaning against the Slingshot, and I was resting up for another try. Mr. Cortina was adding up some figures on a sheet Lou had given him and then began mumbling. I had to grin, because although Mr. Cortina was the best trapeze catcher in the world, he couldn't do numbers as well as *I* could.

Finally he looked up at Lou and said, "As close as I can figure it, Lou, we got the trapeze act all sewed up."

"That's right, Thomas." Lou nodded. Mr. Cortina seemed to listen to him more than to anyone else. "And I promise you, I'll win the prize for the best clown act—with the Magic Yo-Yo. But it's not enough."

"Yes," he agreed sadly, gazing at the sheet. "It's good, but we need more if we are to save the show."

Lou leaned over and tapped the pad with his blunt forefinger. "I *think* Rex will win. There's a new tiger act that Hunter has worked up with the Patmore Circus, but it's not as good as Rex's."

"Even if Rex comes through," he said, shaking his head, "it will not be enough. Will it, Lou?"

The midget stared at the page and finally said, "If we're goin' to save the show, we *gotta* win the New Act Award!"

That was the *big* one worth twenty thousand dollars! We all knew that Milo Hunter had something up his sleeve just to be sure that Thomas Cortina didn't win enough prize money to save the show.

"If we could just be sure of winning *that one,*" Lou said, "we'd be all right!"

"I know how you can make sure of that!"

We all looked around. It was Juan, his face scratched but smiling. He looked at me, then back at the two men. "I can tell you how to make *sure* you win the big money!"

Mr. Cortina and Lou looked at each other, then Mr. Cortina said, "How is that?"

Juan shrugged his muscular shoulders and waved toward the Slingshot. "This is good, no question about that. But it needs a *finish,* you know?"

"What sort of a finish, Juan?" Mr. Cortina asked quickly.

Juan was smooth. He shrugged his shoulders again and smiled. "Why, I'm surprised you haven't thought of it, Thomas. It's a good act, but what if the flier goes through a hoop of fire for a finale?"

I could see it would be the best act in the circus, at least for a season.

Mr. Cortina's face brightened, then he shook his head. "It would be fantastic, Juan, but Barney could never do that sort of act! No beginner could!"

Juan turned toward me. His eyes held a glint Mr. Cortina and Lou missed. I could tell he wanted to get back at me for having made him look bad in front of Angel in the woods.

"No." He smiled. "Barney cannot do it, but *I* can!"

It caught Mr. Cortina and Lou at the same time.

It would be simple for Juan to do the act. He had done more complicated things than that already. But for Barney Buck? Not a chance!

There was only one thing to do, and I did it.

"Juan's right!" I said, swallowing a lump in my throat. "He can do that act, and it'll win the Grand Prize!"

"It's *your* act, Barney!" Mr. Cortina protested.

"Sure!" Lou added. "You own the Slingshot!"

I realized that if I said a word, I could do the act. They were all looking at me, and Mr. Cortina and Lou would never take Juan up on the offer unless I backed off.

There was a real *honor* in these men, something you didn't find every day in the week. They knew that Juan could win that prize and save their circus, but they wouldn't go beyond my word.

All I had to say was "Hey, Mr. Cortina, I guess I can handle it," and that would have been it. I stood there, wanting to do it, wanting the applause and the limelight and everybody patting me on the back. Nobody would ever fault me for doing it. But I couldn't do it!

Mr. Cortina, Lou, and all the other performers were depending on the act. As much as I wanted to say that I'd take care of the Slingshot, I finally shook my head and said, "Juan will have to do it."

To give them credit, Mr. Cortina and Lou tried to talk me out of it. After all, they said, the Buck brothers had invented the act and I'd learned to do it.

"No," I said, "the show is more important than any one member."

Finally, Mr. Cortina put his arm around me and made me look up into his dark eyes. "Barney, you are a good boy. Not many could step aside and let another have the spotlight."

Lou didn't say anything, but his face glowed, and he

gave me a hard punch in the thigh. That meant he approved of what I'd decided.

Word got around, and everybody was really excited about the act. Juan did it right off.

The first time he did the Slingshot, he arced up gracefully, made a beautiful, long curve, and went through the blazing hoop like he'd been doing it for a lifetime! I applauded with the rest.

After everyone had gone to bed, I couldn't fall asleep. I got up, dressed, and walked over to the Big Top. I guess I was thinking about the cheers I'd never hear and feeling a little sorry for myself. All of a sudden I heard somebody say, "Barney, is that you?"

I whirled around. "Dee Dee, what're you doing up at this hour?" I whispered. She came up to me.

"Barney, I heard about your letting Juan do your act."

"Well, shoot! It just makes sense, Dee Dee."

"Maybe so, but I can't think of anyone besides you doing it."

"Lots of people would."

"No, not circus people and not anyone, I guess." It was quiet in the Big Top. Then she moved in close enough for me to see her eyes. "Most people don't give up their act—they hang onto it until they die."

"Well, Juan can do it better than I can, and it's better for the circus." Just then Rajah roared, and Dee Dee came even closer.

124

She shook her blonde hair and whispered, "No, people aren't like that! Most people stake out a place and fight for it. Animals are like that. They want what's theirs!"

I shrugged and stepped back from her. She was getting so close it made me nervous, but she didn't seem to realize it. "Well, I had to let Juan do it, Dee Dee. It's best for the circus."

"You're really a nice boy, Barney!" Dee Dee breathed. Then she took my hand. "You're my best friend, did you know that?"

What was this power I had over girls? *I must use it only for good!* I thought. Then I laughed. "Dee Dee, have you ever thought I may be just a coward? Imagine going up in the air like that and missing!"

She thought about it, then shook her head. "No, you're not a coward, Barney. You're just . . . " She stopped and turned her head without finishing. Suddenly she whispered, "Someone's coming!"

Pulling away from me, she turned and ran away. I stood there for a long time wondering if I was a Christian martyr or a wimp!

11
Accusation

Two weeks rolled by. It was hard to believe that Joe, Jake, and I would be back home to Goober Holler in another few days! There wasn't any need for us to go to the Super Circus, now that I wasn't going to do the Slingshot act.

When I watched Juan doing it, it should have made me feel better, but it really didn't. I guess I wanted to go to New York and pull off that stunt more than I'd ever wanted to do anything in my whole life. I even prayed about it a little, but my prayers sounded selfish even to me, so I didn't really expect God to take any action.

Every evening I went over to help Angel, but by this time we weren't making any effort to study. Most of the time we just talked or made fudge or listened to the stereo. She liked country western, but I made her listen to other stuff just to give my ears a rest.

On the Thursday night of our final week, Lou came by. As usual he and Mr. Cortina figured up the bills and hoped things would look better. They never did, though. Finally I heard Mr. Cortina say, "Well, we can only enter five competitions. That's the rule. And we must win at least four of them to scrape by." Lou shook his head. "Not going to be easy, Thomas. I been rapping with some clowns from other outfits. They're all going to go for broke on this one. And you know as well as me, *every* circus has got at least one good act. I don't see how we can make it."

Mr. Cortina slapped his hand against his leg and said loudly, "We just have to. That's all, Lou! It's the only way!"

"Well, if we get the big one, the New Act Award, even if we miss on a couple of the others, I think we can make it. And it looks good to me. That Juan—he's a pain in the neck sometimes like all fliers, but I gotta admit he flies like a bird!"

"Best since Felipe when he was flying," Mr. Cortina said.

"I think he'll win it for us," Lou said. "But what a swelled head he'll have then!"

Juan had been coming to the trailer a lot, but he had

never stayed long. He would make fun of the "kid stuff" Angel and I did, then go prowling off. Usually he'd go into the nearest town, and I knew he sometimes got into hot water, but he was so good at his act Mr. Cortina let him get by with it.

The next day, I clambered up into the rigging and set up the hoop so Juan could do his Thread the Needle bit. I was so good at getting around high up in the tent that I never thought about it anymore.

I set the hoop on fire and sat down with my legs dangling off the perch to watch the act. I'd never seen it without a thrill, and I knew it couldn't miss. Juan said, "All right," and I heard the *whirrrr-thump* the Slingshot made. Then Juan left the ground like an arrow, rising with his arms out in front of him, his head held back, and his toes pointed like a dancer.

Then suddenly I knew something was wrong! I had a good angle of the view, and I let out a holler, but there was nothing I could do. Maybe, though, my cry did some good, because Mr. Cortina, who was on the far side of the net from the Slingshot, straightened up and saw me waving my arm toward Juan, who was coming like a bullet.

Juan was going to overshoot the burning hoop, and if he did that, it meant he wasn't going to hit the net right. I had the crazy thought of trying to grab him as he went by, but that was nutty. He sailed over my head, grazing the top of the hoop. I saw his eyes open wide and knew he'd seen what was happening, but there wasn't much he could do.

Mr. Cortina backed away from the net, then Juan doubled up and tried to shorten the distance. But he hit way too far toward the end of the net, and it threw him up and over the edge. It was exactly what had happened to Felipe years ago, but I was afraid it might do worse than cripple Juan—it might kill him!

I held on to the rigging as if paralyzed while Juan went up, his arms and legs awkward for once. Then he arced over, his body headed straight for the hard-packed earth!

I said one of my instant prayers and then saw Mr. Cortina getting underneath. He watched Juan come down, just like a baseball player watches a high fly that's heading toward him.

It was amazing, but he stopped him! When Juan came down on him, he collapsed, strong as he was. He got up almost at once, and so did Juan, but he was holding his arm as if it was broken.

I scrambled down and by the time I got to Juan and Mr. Cortina, a crowd had gathered around them. Mr. Cortina was touching Juan's arm. "I think it's broken!" Juan said.

"Lillian! Get him to the hospital. I'll be there as soon as I can." Mrs. Cortina followed her husband's advice and led Juan away, his face drawn in pain. Mr. Cortina had a hard look on his face. He walked over to the Sling-shot, where Joe sat in shock.

"What happened, Joe? You promised that there would be nothing like this—ever!"

Joe's lips trembled and he began to stutter. Joe was very sensitive, and whenever he got upset, it was hard for him to talk.

"Let me talk to him, Mr. Cortina," I said. "Hey, Joe, don't worry. Juan's all right. It's not your fault."

"But . . . I don't understand . . . ," he started to say in a tight voice. Then he did a double take at the simple panel on the side of the Slingshot.

"What is it, Joe?" I asked.

"Look at that screw. Somebody messed with it, see?"

I looked carefully and noticed the head of the screw seemed chewed up as if someone had used the wrong-sized screwdriver on it. "What does that mean?"

Joe pulled a screwdriver out of his pocket and removed the screw, then studied the panel. "Somebody readjusted the tension-setting gauge," he said. "See, if you move this gauge like this, the reading won't be set with the distance. Somebody messed the gauge up. That's why Juan didn't come down right!"

"The Phantom!" Lou whispered, but Jake just shook his head.

"If a ghost did it, it'll be the first time a ghost ever got caught in the act," Jake said.

"What do you mean, Jake?" Mr. Cortina asked.

Jake was scrambling up on one of the shorter tent poles and pulling at something I couldn't see. "Joe and Lou and me figured that sooner or later the Phantom was gonna have another shot at doing something dirty. So Joe rigged up three cameras, and we put them up every night."

"Right!" Joe nodded. "I figured he'd try either the generator, the animals, or the Slingshot. So we set a camera with a trip wire in all three places. Did it make a picture, Jake?"

"Sure did!" Jake came sliding down the pole with an old Polaroid camera in his hands. "Even in the dim light we should've gotten *something!*"

"Can you check it now?" I asked.

"Sure!" Jake said, pulling a tab down and fiddling with the camera. "The photo's just about developed." He stared at it, then suddenly handed it to Mr. Cortina. "There's your phantom, Mr. Cortina. With his hand right in the till!"

The circus owner took it, stared at it, then slowly raised his head. "Rex, you better explain this."

A wave seemed to part the people around Rex Rogers, who suddenly looked scared. Mr. Cortina walked right up to him and showed him the picture. "You are the Phantom, Rex."

"No!" he said in a high-pitched voice, not loud and

scratchy like it usually was. "No, Thomas, I swear to you I had nothing to do with what happened."

Felipe came to stand beside his brother, Thomas, and I noticed a hard glint in his eyes. "I have known it was you for a long time, Rex. Every time an 'accident' happened, you were not far away."

"What about this picture?" Lou growled. "You can't deny that, now can you?"

An angry mutter ran around the crowd. Several men clenched their fists and took a step toward the animal trainer, who was looking more and more frightened all the time.

"You're a murderer," I said, staring at him. "Juan could have been killed, and a lot of others, if that fire you started had gotten out of control!"

I think he would have been stormed right then, but Mr. Cortina pushed his muscular frame between him and a man who was about to swing on him with a tent peg. "No! I will not have this! I will take care of this man." The crowd settled down, growling like a dog that's been cheated out of its dinner. "You probably will not go to jail. Even this picture will not be enough. But I promise you this—you will never work in a circus again. I promise you!"

Rex Rogers was a strong man, but now his face was twitching and his hands trembled as he touched his chin. He tried to swallow, then whispered, "Thomas, the circus is my *life*. It's all I know! Don't do this to me!"

I'd always thought Thomas Cortina had one of the nicest faces I'd ever seen, but he looked downright cruel as he fixed Rex Rogers with his eyes and said in a deadly voice, "You are a killer! I will see to it you never work again!"

Suddenly Dee Dee was there, her face wet with tears. She ran to her father and threw her arms around him. "I know you didn't do it, Daddy! You didn't! You didn't!"

Mr. Cortina shook his head, then said in a gentler voice, "Nobody will love you any less, Dee Dee, but your father must answer for what he has done."

Rex Rogers turned like a caged animal and might have done something he'd regret, but Ruth Stratton—the one person in the whole troupe who'd ever gone out of her way to be friendly to him—followed him. She didn't say a word, but when he saw her, he had a strangely happy look on his face. Maybe he realized that at least one other person besides Dee Dee didn't hate him.

"Come on, Lou," Mr. Cortina said. "Let's get to the hospital." They left in a hurry, and the rest of us just stood around and talked about the whole thing.

Most of us were saying things like "He ought to go to jail," but I noticed Angel wasn't saying much of anything. She kept looking over at Rex Rogers' trailer and biting her lip.

"What's the matter, Angel?" I asked. "You mad about Juan?"

"Oh, I'm sorry for Juan, but I'm happy he didn't get badly hurt. It's him and Dee Dee I worry about."

She glanced at the trailer again, and I shook my head. "Dee Dee, yes. Rex Rogers, no! He's not worth it, Angel."

"Maybe not, but he's so alone, Barney! I don't think he has a friend in the world, except for Ruth."

"Well, why should he?" It bothered me to see her so mixed up. "Why *should* he have any friends? He's a mean old grouch!"

"He wasn't always that way," Angel said, staring at me. "Before his wife died, he was always real nice. He would take Dee Dee and me to the movies every Saturday when we were little, and he was always a help to anybody in the circus who was in trouble." She looked at the people standing around. "I see some here that Rex pulled out of a jam or two."

"You must be imagining stuff, Angel. I never heard anyone say anything nice about him."

"I think he's like that because he's scared or guilty."

"Guilty? About being the Phantom?"

"No, of course not!" Angel snapped. She bit her lip and shook her head. "His wife was such a pretty thing, a little like Dee Dee. She was part of the act, and had no fear of the cats at all. They were all just kittens to her. But . . ."

"What happened?"

"Well, I don't remember it too well, but the story is that Rex let her go into a cage with a bad cat and she was killed. They say he didn't say a word for six months, and never a kind word after that. I think he's still blaming himself for that."

"You might be right, and that may be a very good reason why he's trying to destroy the circus."

She stared at me. "Why do you say that?"

"Maybe he blames the whole circus for the death of his wife. I know that's nutty, and so do you, but maybe he *is* nutty. It's possible."

"I suppose, but I can't believe it."

We talked about it for about an hour and a half. Then Angel's father and Lou came back, looking serious. "He's all right," Mr. Cortina said at once. Angel gave a deep sigh of relief. "His arm is not broken, just badly bruised. He will be all right in a couple of weeks."

"Oh, that's wonderful!" Angel cried out. "Can I go see him, Daddy?"

"Tomorrow," he said. "Of course, we have to be glad for that, but the other side of the picture isn't so good."

"Oh," I said suddenly, "that means he won't be able to do the Slingshot act in New York."

"It's worse than that, Barney," Lou broke in. He pulled his floppy hat off and punched it with his fist, then threw it on the ground. "We not only have no Sling-shot act, we have no animal act."

I'd forgotten that they'd depended on Rex Rogers to win big at the Super Circus. My stomach hurt to think about it. "But what can you do?" I asked.

"Do?" Mr. Cortina grunted. "Nothing left to *do*. No sense even going without our two main acts. All I have to do is sign a paper. Then Hunter owns this circus lock, stock, and barrel."

I guess we were all stunned. I know I'd always been sure that everything would come out all right. You might say I had had faith in it. Coach had always been telling me to believe God for stuff, and I'd done that, but God had fallen down on the job! At least, that's what it looked like to me at the time!

That night when we finally went to bed, Felipe and I tried to be cheerful. He was moving slowly like an old man, and I finally asked him, "Felipe, what will you do if the circus folds?"

He laughed, but not like it was funny. "Oh, I can always get a job, Barney. A good clown can catch on. Even Hunter has offered me a top spot—not that I'd take it. It's Thomas I'm worried about. I'm alone, but he has a family to think about. I'm not sure he can handle it."

"He's just got to, doesn't he, Felipe?"

He was quiet for a long time before he finally

answered me. "Sure, he's got to handle it. But when you take a hard fall, not everybody can get up and try again."

"But *you* did!"

After another long pause, he said, "Sure, *I* did, but you see, Barney, Thomas has never *had* a fall. He's always had good things happen. He got Lillian and Angel and owns this circus. Now I'll tell you one thing. When a guy has it good all his life and *then* takes a fall, *that's* when he can really get hurt!"

I couldn't think of any answer to that, so I tried to tell God about it. He sure seemed a long way off that night!

12
Coach in a Corner

DOORS! Doors! They're coming in!" Lou hollered. All of a sudden it hit me that this was Home Sweet Home, the last performance of the season. And probably the last ever as far as the Buck boys were concerned.

Coach had driven down from Cedarville to take us home. He was sitting in the *blues,* the cheapest seats in the Big Top.

I watched pretty carefully since I wasn't likely to see it like this again, and I did the Slingshot act, too—not Threading the Needle, which Juan could do so well. Just the Big Jump.

Finally it was over. Mr. Cortina said we didn't have to stay around to help take the tent down and load it up.

I got all packed up, and even though it was late, I knew Coach would be in the cook tent. There was always a big feed after Home Sweet Home, and when I got there, almost everybody was there. Usually this would have been a really happy party, but nobody was laughing much.

When I got to the long wooden table where Coach was sitting with Jake and Joe on one side and the Cortinas across from him, everyone was talking about Rex Rogers.

"I tell you, Thomas, you're letting him off too easy!" Dailey Sanders, one of the canvas men, shouted. "He ought to be locked up!"

"Where is he anyway?" someone asked. "He's probably run away by this time."

"No, I've been keeping an eye on the trailer," Felipe said. "He's still in there all right."

It went on and on, and finally I stuck in my two cents' worth. "I'd like to load *him* into the Slingshot and shoot him clear into the middle of the Pacific Ocean!"

"Would you really, Barney?" Coach asked.

"Sure, I would!" Actually, I didn't want to do that. But since everybody, except Angel, was mad at him, it just seemed easier to chime in with them.

I hadn't noticed Dee Dee when she came in, but suddenly she was standing there and I realized that she'd heard me. Without a word she began to cry and ran back to the trailer.

"Nice work, Barney!" Angel said. "I hope you enjoyed that!"

"Well, for cryin' out loud," I said. "Why are you picking on *me?* Everybody else is knocking the guy!"

"But you're supposed to be the big *Christian,* Barney," Angel answered right back. "And I don't see much to all that stuff if you're any example."

"Nobody could forgive a rotten guy like *that!*" I cried. I was mad, especially when everybody in the whole tent had stopped eating and talking and was staring at me. I felt like I was on trial or something!

"You sure don't learn fast, do you, Barney?" Coach said. He reached into his pocket and pulled out a battered old New Testament and flipped it open. He could tell I was a little embarrassed, but he started reading anyway:

> And when they were come to the place, which is called Calvary, there they crucified him, and the malefactors, one on the right hand, and the other on the left. Then said Jesus, "Father, forgive them, for they know not what they do."

When you get caught in a wrong position, you have to holler, so I did! "Aw, well, sure, Coach. But that was *Jesus!* What I meant was that nobody else but him would forgive a rotten person!"

He gave me a hard look, and I flinched. Then he turned a few pages and read:

> And they stoned Stephen, calling upon God, and saying, "Lord Jesus, receive my spirit." And he kneeled down and cried with a loud voice, "Lord, lay not this sin to their charge."

He put the New Testament back into his pocket and stared at me. I just muttered, "But that's hard, Coach!"

"Did you ever read anywhere in the Bible that it was easy to be a Christian?"

"But I thought the preacher said it was all free," Angel said.

"Oh, it's easy to become a Christian," Coach said with a smile. "It's another thing to behave like the person Jesus wants you to be."

"I don't get that," Lou said in a puzzled voice.

"Well, are you married, Lou?"

"Sure."

"How long did it take you to *get* married?"

"About five minutes," he said with a wide grin. "But it took twenty years for me to become what those five minutes made me." Everyone nearby laughed.

"I don't know, Mr. Littlejohn," Angel said, her face suddenly serious looking. "It seems impossible to do some of the things Jesus said. Like loving your enemies."

"Barney ought to be able to tell you about that," Coach replied. "He taught a bunch of younger kids all about dealing with your enemies, at a camp last fall."

My face turned red, making the scar on my forehead stand out. I looked like a torch on a skinny stick with my stupid red hair, but I sure knew what he was saying.

"I guess I better go get packed," I mumbled, starting to leave the table.

"Hold on a minute, Barney!" Coach said. "Don't forget we're leaving tomorrow right after breakfast. I'm staying at Bartlett's Motel down the road, if you need me for anything sooner."

"Yes sir," I said hastily, then turned and headed straight for Felipe's trailer. When I got there, I unpacked my stuff and repacked it, just so I wouldn't be caught telling a lie about packing!

I didn't want to talk to anybody, so I pulled off my clothes and went to bed. I must've laid there for a couple of hours. After a while, I heard people leaving the cook tent. Coach didn't come after me, as I thought he might, so I breathed a sigh of relief. He must've decided to spend some time with Joe and Jake before going back to his motel. We could've left for Cedarville right away, but we'd convinced him to let us have one more day with the Cortina Brothers' Circus.

Eventually Felipe came in and went to bed. Everything was quiet, and I must've dozed off after awhile. But even in my sleep I kept hearing Coach read those words: "'Forgive them, for they know not what they do.'"

That old Rex Rogers knew exactly what he was doing! I thought angrily.

How do you know? The question popped into my mind like a gentle ripple in a pond.

Well, he just did! I snapped back.

So, you never did anything wrong, Barney, the Pure One?

Was it my conscience or the Lord giving me these uncomfortable thoughts? Actually, I was too mad to find out.

"Shut up! Will you just shut up!" I said out loud.

Finally I went to sleep and had the worst nightmare I'd ever had in my life. I dreamed I'd done something *awful,* and I was in this big room, standing up on a pillar, and millions of people were staring at me. They pointed at me and said, "Guilty! Guilty!" Then somebody started chanting, "Kill him! Kill him!"

I looked everywhere for even one friend, but there wasn't one. Finally the crowd started rushing at me. That woke me up. I was drenched with sweat and trembling like a leaf!

I knew what I had to do, but it took me an hour of struggling to decide to do it. When it was over, I slipped out of the trailer and made my way in the darkness to Rex Rogers' trailer and tapped on the door.

I guess he and Dee Dee were asleep, but I kept knocking until a light went on inside and he opened the door a crack. "Who's there?"

"It's me, Mr. Rogers, Barney Buck."

"What do *you* want?" he said, starting to slam the door.

"Wait a minute, Mr. Rogers!" I said quickly. "I have to talk to you. Please let me come in, and I promise I'll leave in just a few minutes. But I gotta tell you something."

He stood there without saying anything, and I thought he would slam the door, but he didn't. He finally pulled it open and I went inside. He turned a table lamp on, and Dee Dee came in wearing a long pink robe.

"Barney! What are you doing here this time of night?" she asked.

"Well, I have something to tell your dad—and you, too, Dee Dee."

"Come to tell me I'm a murderer?" Rex Rogers said. He looked pretty awful. He hadn't shaved and hadn't slept much either, judging from the bags under his eyes.

"No sir, I . . . I came to tell you I'm sorry I said what I said, and I want you to forgive me."

He stared at me, then finally asked in a hoarse voice, "Do you mean you don't think I did it?"

I thought about that, then shook my head. "I'll level

with you, Mr. Rogers. I don't know if you're the Phantom or not. But even if you are, I had no right to pitch into you that way. And I just came to tell you I'm sorry, and . . . and I'd like to be your friend."

It got so quiet all I could hear was Dee Dee sniffling. Then she threw her arms around his neck and said, "See, Daddy! I told you it would be all right. People will believe you."

He stared at me. Then the tense muscles in his face relaxed, and he nodded. "That's . . . that's what I'd like, Barney. I need a friend. And now I want to ask you something. Have you been meeting Dee Dee at night?"

"Well, we met a few times about a month ago, but Dee Dee and I knew it wasn't right. So that was it. All we did was talk about English and stuff."

He stared at me, then sighed. "You know what I was doing at the Slingshot the night it was wrecked, Barney? Trying to catch you and Dee Dee."

"Daddy, I was with Ruth!" Dee Dee said excitedly. "That's where I've been most every night."

He nodded. "I wish I'd known that. I didn't even touch that Slingshot, Barney. I must have tripped the wire, so whoever *did* do the job came after I was there."

"I wish you'd known about me and Ruth, Daddy." Dee Dee gave him a shy look. "I wish you'd go with me when I go see her."

"Oh, Dee Dee, Ruth's a young woman. She wouldn't want an old man like me in the way."

"Yes, she would! She said so!" Dee Dee said quickly. "She . . . she really *likes* you!"

It seemed to be a puzzle to him. "She does? I can't think of why. I haven't been anything much to like the last few years."

"I know you've been having a hard time, but Ruth is smart. She can see what you're really like under all that bluster." Dee Dee smiled and gave him a kiss.

"Well, I'll think about that, but first I have to clear my name. Barney, I didn't have a thing to do with that criminal act!"

"Well, I believe you, Mr. Rogers. And I think if you tell Mr. Cortina and the others what you've told me, they'll believe you, too. At least some of them."

He wouldn't agree for a long time. I think he didn't want people to know how suspicious he'd been about me and Dee Dee, but she talked him into it. "You go first thing in the morning, Daddy. You hear?"

The next morning after breakfast, I got the circus people together. When you're going to make a donkey out of yourself like I was planning to do, you might as well get a crowd together to watch you do it! Juan was there with his arm in a sling.

First, Rex Rogers told his story, and sure enough,

146

some of them believed him and some didn't. Mr. Cortina did, I could tell, and that was a big step.

After the hubbub died down, I said, "You know, lots of times my brother Jake has said, 'Barney, wait until you hear my plan.' In every case I can think of, it's either cost me money or blood."

Jake ducked his head. "Aw, shucks!" he said as if he'd done a big thing.

"Well, Mr. Cortina, wait till you hear my plan!" I said.

"It better be good," Lou said. "I feel like we're arranging the deck chairs on the *Titanic!*"

"Look, if you'll let Rex Rogers go to New York and do his act, that leaves only the Slingshot, right?" I said.

Mr. Cortina saw where I was going. "Ah, that's what you want to do? But it's no good, Barney. The Big Jump is fine for around here, but the Super Circus is a different league."

"Well, I'm saying that if Juan coaches me, I'll try to Thread the Needle!"

They all stared at me and a few snorted, but most of them just shook their heads. Mr. Cortina said, "That's a fine offer, Barney, but in the first place, Coach Littlejohn would never let you do it."

"Sure, he would. He'd just about have to!"

"I would, would I?" Coach said, approaching the group. His jaw got hard like it did when he felt challenged. "Why would I *have* to, tell me that?" Everyone turned to look at him.

"Because I'm doing it for a friend," I said, "and you're always saying what the Bible says, 'A friend sticks closer than a brother.' Now isn't that what you always say?"

Coach began to shift around, and this time *he* was the one getting red. "Aw, Barney, this is different! Why, it's dangerous. You could get killed."

I had him then! He was always getting me with his Bible quotations. This time I pulled his black New Testament out of his pocket and read a verse. I have to admit I'd looked it up the night before, but he didn't know that. "It says here, 'Greater love hath no man than this, that a man lays down his life for his friends.'" I put the Testament back and looked him right in the eye. "Coach, I wanna know if this stuff out of the Bible you've been teaching me is just Sunday school *talk,* or does it really count out here in the real world with real people?"

Now Coach was squirming, and I knew if I was ever going to get to do that act, both Coach and Mr. Cortina had to agree. Finally Coach said, "Sure, Barney, but you can't just take chances without any concern. The devil told Jesus to throw himself off the high part of the temple, but Jesus told him that would be tempting God."

I was ready for him again. "But Mr. Cortina and Juan are going to teach me. I'm not too bad anyway, and with their help we can do it." I played my strongest argument. "It's the only way Mr. Cortina is going to keep his circus, Coach. That's why I want to do it. And I have faith that it'll be all right, don't you?"

Coach stared at me, and it got real quiet. Then he grinned. "You stinker! You got me into this, didn't you? Even your own brother Jake couldn't have done it any smoother."

"I can do it then?" I asked.

"Far as I'm concerned," he said with a shrug. "You realize what my intended bride and your future mother will do to me, but let it fall on my head. It's up to you, Thomas."

Every head turned toward Thomas Cortina, who was staring at me. Finally he said, "I have never seen an angel, but if you can save my circus, Barney Buck, I will tell the world that you are one. Juan, will you help with the clumsy angel we have here?"

Juan looked at me like I was a strange animal from another world. Then he finally smiled and said, "You must have led a full life, Barney, to be so willing to give it up. But I will do my best to see that you don't wind up in a box."

That was good news! I'd been worried about Juan. Then my brother Jake piped up. "I've been thinking, Mr. Cortina. Why don't we give Barney some kind of coating that burns—like kerosene—and then he can ignite as he goes through the hoop, and say, then we could have this big tank of water instead of a net. . . ."

My dear brother Jake—always looking out to raise me up in the world any way he could!

I didn't say anything, because my *real* plan was even wackier than his!

13
The Daring Young Man

COACH left for Cedarville, and I practiced with the Slingshot until noon with Mr. Cortina and Juan coaching me. They just about dropped their teeth when I made a perfect shot at Threading the Needle on the third try! I didn't do it gracefully like Juan, but I went right on through!

Actually it wasn't all that hard. Joe had the Slingshot lined up just right, and as long as I kept my body straight and didn't wiggle around, I shot right through. It wasn't any higher than I'd gone before, and making the fall afterward was just the same.

"Great! You're a winner," Juan said. I don't know why his getting hurt had made him like me better. I guess he liked it that I was willing to risk my neck for his act.

Mr. Cortina was beaming like the sun, but I said, "You know, you're still not going to make it. I mean, you were really counting on your own act to tilt the scales in your favor."

He winced and shrugged. "Well, that is true, but there is nothing to be done. It's in the hands of God."

"Well, we can put 'foots' on our prayers, as the man said," I commented.

"How do you mean, Barney?" Juan smiled. "Do you have another idea?"

"Yes, and you won't like it!" I said.

"Try me out," Juan said. "Couldn't be any sillier than Threading the Needle."

"You don't think so?" I said with a grin. "Then how about this? Suppose you're up there on your bar, Mr. Cortina, and suppose the Slingshot shoots me right to you, and suppose you catch me just like you do Juan? Suppose all *that!*"

"Suppose the moon is made of cheese!" Mr. Cortina grinned. He thought I was joking, but then he took one look at me. "You can't be serious, Barney."

"I'm serious as measles."

"But . . . but . . . it's *impossible!*" he sputtered. "Tell him it can't be done, Juan! Tell this child what he wants to do is impossible."

Juan stared at me, then shook his head. "I don't know that it is."

"But you know you started practicing when you were three years old," Mr. Cortina said, a look of exasperation all over his face.

"Sure, but I don't have to do all the things *he* does," I said. "No somersaults, no fancy stuff. I just let Joe pull the trigger, I go, and then either you catch me or you don't." I gave him a smile. "See, it's an administrative problem, Mr. Cortina!"

He laughed, but I could see a tiny light flickering in his eyes. "You know, it just might work. With Juan it would work, but, no, it's too dangerous."

"That's *his* problem." Juan smiled. I didn't mind, because I knew he was kidding. "I say, let's give it a shot. I tell you this, Thomas, if he can do it, we're home free! No way anybody is going to top an act like that!"

"You're right there!" Mr. Cortina slapped his hands together. "All right, we will begin. We have only three days, then we have to move to New York. Come, let us talk to Joe. You must not go too fast—and not too slow. You must reach the peak of your climb just as I am coming back to pick you up. Timing! Timing! All is in the timing."

Well, I wish I could tell you that it went smooth as silk, but it didn't. As a matter of fact, it didn't go at all!

We tried and tried, but it never really quite came off. Part of the reason was *me*. Somehow getting caught by Mr. Cortina was a lot different than just going up and falling into the net. It meant I couldn't really make a good turn. I had to keep straight and reach up to Mr. Cortina's hands, and I just didn't trust him! It was that simple.

Juan understood. "I've been that way many times. Oh, not for years, but when I first started. Your life is in the hands of the catcher. If you have one ounce of doubt, you'll flinch and the catch will go bad. You have to believe in those hands! You have to believe that if the tent catches on fire, if an elephant breaks loose, if there is an earthquake—none of that will matter. Thomas's hands will still be there and they will not let you fall!"

For three days we tried, and it wasn't all my fault. "This machine is good," Mr. Cortina said, patting the Slingshot after we'd come close twice in a row. "But there are too many variables. Just a fraction off and it's no-catch! Fine for going into the net, but whether we can ever do it or not, I don't know. I don't think so. Next year Juan and I will have lots of time, maybe then."

"But the Super Circus . . . ," I said.

"We'll just hope Threading the Needle will be enough." But he didn't seem to believe it and neither did Juan or Lou.

"If only . . . ," Juan said.

Lou made a face. "The *if onlys* will always be with us," he said.

We left for New York, leaving at the last possible

moment, and the trip was a blur to me. I slept a lot of the time, and the rest of the time Angel, Dee Dee, Juan, and I played games in Juan's motor home.

I'd never been to New York, and we didn't have time to see any of it. We couldn't pitch tents on the streets, so we stayed at a Holiday Inn. Madison Square Garden was huge. All of a sudden the idea of doing *anything* in a place that big froze me up. I knew I wouldn't be able to *spit* with those huge spotlights on me, much less do something as hard as that flying act.

We had a good night's rest and went to the Garden the next day to set up our rigging. We had plenty of extra help, but we checked it again and again.

It was about noon when Milo Hunter arrived. I'd never been near him before. He was pretty impressive. He was a big man and wore sharp clothes. His white suit probably cost as much as a good redbone hound back home. The diamond on his finger would have paid for the football program back home at Ouachita Baptist University!

He had a big, booming voice, and I thought he'd probably been a ringmaster—which he had been. "Well, here you are, my friend Thomas!" He smiled like a great white shark and gave Mr. Cortina a fat-looking hand. "I suppose you're here to win the money to pay old Milo off, am I right?"

"You are right," Mr. Cortina said without a smile. "And when I do, I'll never be in debt to you again."

"Now, Thomas, that's not kind! Haven't I offered to buy your show many times, and at a good profit?"

"You will not get this one, Milo," Mr. Cortina said. "We didn't come here to lose."

"Well, certainly not." He laughed. "And I take it this is the famous daring young man who Threads the Needle, eh?"

It took even Mr. Cortina off guard. He blinked, and that tickled Hunter. "Oh, I have my little ways of keeping up with you, Thomas. And I understand he's very good! Maybe you might even like to join one of my shows, eh, Barney?"

"No, thank you."

He didn't like the way I shut him off. I could tell that beneath the grin he wasn't anything but a wolf!

"Well, have it your own way, my boy, but one last offer, Thomas. I know you have had some difficulties, and I'm ready now to make one final offer. There is no chance you can win enough out of this venture to pay off your note, but I'll do this. I'll raise my last offer by ten thousand dollars, and you'll get to stay on as manager at a considerable salary. Now you can't say fairer than that, can you? Come on. How about it?"

"Milo," Mr. Cortina said. He sounded so positive Hunter thought he was about to say yes and began pulling a contract out of his inner pocket. "I'll tell you the truth, I'd clean sewers before I'd work for you."

I never saw a man get so worked up! Hunter's face turned red as a tomato. "You'll get *nothing!*" he began to scream. I thought he'd have a heart attack before somebody led him away. "Do you hear me! *Nothing!*" Some people then pulled him away by force.

"Now, let's get in some practice," Mr. Cortina said as if nothing had happened.

But we didn't get any practice to speak of. Reporters were all over the place, getting in the way and keeping the performers busy. The Super Circus had caught the fancy of the public, and every seat was sold. There was even going to be a TV special about it.

One of the stars on a prime-time talk show came around with a bunch of cameramen, showing off and cracking jokes. I hadn't thought he was funny on TV, and in real person he acted like a nerd.

He made a few jokes in bad taste when he was talking to Mr. Cortina. Then he turned to me. "And what's your thing? You a snake charmer? You're lean and long enough to be one, aren't you now?" Some of the crewmen laughed, but I just went on helping Felipe test the rigging. My silence irked the man. "You must be a star. You're too stuck-up to be anything else."

He got on Lou's nerves, so Lou piped up and said, "He's just a boy from Arkansas, Harry, trying to help us out. Why don't you go dress up in one of your funny suits and make bad jokes somewhere else? We're busy!"

That made the guy furious. When he went on a TV special the night before the Super Circus started, he really let me have it. I guess somebody had done his homework for him, because he knew where I was from and he had a lot of jokes about hillbillies.

Then he really got to us. He'd pumped somebody and found out about the Slingshot. He even knew about the way we'd tried to make it into a catching act with Thomas Cortina! I had a suspicion that the real phantom must have been passing him notes.

"So what we have here is a red-headed little hill-billy—Mountain William. He's going to let himself be thrown into a net! Oh, he goes through a hoop, but I ask you folks, is *that* show biz? Is that the circus? No, this hayseed is taking up time with the greatest performers on earth, and I, for one, would like the committee to forbid this imposter to parade his pitiful little act in front of this fine audience!"

So there I was in our motel room watching the show and wishing I hadn't. I must have looked pretty sick, because Juan gave me a smile and said, "Who listens to that cluck?"

"About fifty million people!" I said.

"You'll do great, Barney," Angel whispered. "Don't you worry."

"Don't worry, Barney," Jake and Joe said in unison.

Everybody was telling me not to worry, but nobody was telling me *how* to manage that little trick.

The next morning at the Garden, Mr. Cortina was steaming. "A 'committee' just came and told me to take the Slingshot out of the show," he said, "but I told them what they could do."

"Can they make you do it?" Lou asked.

"No! They know I would tell the press about them letting a dumb talk show run this show." He looked unhappy. "What can happen is that they won't give Barney's act a fair look. They already know about it. Half the value is the novelty of it. Now that's gone."

"Not if you catch me," I said. "We have to do the *whole* act, Mr. Cortina!"

"But we've never made it, and we would only have one try."

"And if you don't make the catch, you'll get no votes at all," Juan said.

"I think we don't have any choice," I argued. Not that I *wanted* to argue. I really wanted to go to Goober Holler and hunt coons with Tim and not have to get in those spotlights!

But I continued. "We've got *no* chance if we don't try it. We have a small chance if we do. I say we do it."

Lou laughed. "Son, you should have been born in a circus. You're a real trouper. I vote for you!"

"Do it, Dad," Angel said. She gave me a squeeze, which I pretended not to notice.

Finally Mr. Cortina said, "You're right, Barney. We

won't lose for lack of trying. Lou, Felipe, get the bar set up to do the Catch."

So there I was, asking to do a trick that had never been done in front of fifty thousand people, with a 99 percent chance of either making a perfect fool out of myself or breaking my neck!

"Cheer up, Barney," Jake said. "If you get lucky, you'll break your neck Threading the Needle, so you won't even have to try the Catch!"

"Sure, Jake, that's right," I said, looking up into the top of Madison Square Garden. "I forgot that behind every silver lining, there's a dark cloud. Just keep on keeping my spirits up!"

14

What Goes Up Must Come Down

EVERY seat was packed that night! I was glad we'd
practiced Threading the Needle a couple of hours
earlier. It gave me a better feel for the real thing coming
up. Still, as I glanced around into the sea of faces, I
didn't feel any less nervous! Even Juan and Mr. Cortina
were more tense than usual.

Charlton Lancaster, the famous movie star, did a
good job as ringmaster. He'd been an acrobat in his
younger days. Way up high in special seats were the
judges. As the Super Circus went on, I kept looking up
at them and hoping they'd give us a break.

"I know those judges," Lou said as he got ready to
go on. "They're hard but they're fair! They don't care

nothing about what some TV idiot says. They're going to give those prizes to the performers who have the best stuff!"

Those judges had a job! I'd seen a few circuses, but here was the cream! I ran back and forth trying to see as many acts as I could besides helping with the equipment for our people.

What gave me the biggest thrill was to see Rex Rogers looking like a real winner! He and Dee Dee brought the house down with a new wrinkle they'd worked up. *"That's* in the bag, Barney!" Lou said with a wide grin.

Lou was, too, with the Human Yo-Yo act. The judges loved it. I gave Joe a hug. "That's for you, Joe, all that applause! Hear it?"

He gave me a bashful smile. "Sure, but you're going to kill 'em with the Slingshot, Barney, aren't you?"

I wasn't too sure about that! The animal acts and the clown acts were over, and I watched the jugglers, then the high-wire people. It all lasted nearly three hours, but the time for me to go on was rushing at me like an oncoming train. I must have gotten ten drinks of water I was so nervous, until Mr. Cortina growled, "Quit that! You'll be so waterlogged you'll never get off the ground."

Felipe stuck close to me, trying to calm me down. He'd worked real hard with Joe getting all the controls set just right, and he kept patting me on the shoulder

162

and saying, "Don't get uptight, Barney. It's just another show!"

That was like telling a rookie pitcher "Don't worry, kid. It's just another World Series!"

Well, my turn finally came! I was the last act, can you believe it? All the new acts were last, and I didn't even watch because I knew they'd all look so good I'd want to hide in a hole.

"And now, ladeeez and gentlemen," Charlton Lancaster said, "let me introduce the newest member of the circus! Direct from the wilds of Goober Holler, Arkansas, Barney Buck!"

He got a big laugh, and Lou slapped me on the bottom and said, "That helped a lot, kid! They wanna see you do good! Get out there and break a leg!"

I was blinded as I stepped into those spotlights, but the ringmaster gave the whole story about how Joe had invented not only the Slingshot but the Magic Yo-Yo. By the time I'd gotten settled down into the sled, I was feeling a little light-headed, but not completely berserk!

"And now the Human Slingshot will Thread the Needle! Sailing high into the air, he will pass through a hoop no larger than your Aunt Fannie's lower anatomy!"

Everybody laughed, and I nodded at Joe, who looked real tense. Felipe was standing there to double-check, and Joe pulled the trigger!

It was like always, except as I shot off the platform

and rose to the top of the Garden, I glimpsed some movement where Joe and Felipe were standing.

Then I was rising higher and higher, and the music and the drum roll and the lights flashing out of the darkness were all I could think of.

The hoop was there, and I raced toward it like an arrow, keeping my body straight and my head fixed so I could twist or turn in case the Slingshot was a fraction off. That was what we'd worked on for so long, but suddenly I saw that something *was* wrong!

I had only a fraction of a second, but I'd done the act enough so that I could gauge my approach to a split-second edge—and I already knew I was going to be just about one foot too high. I was going to brush the top of the hoop, and that would destroy the success of the stunt. There was no time to really make a decision, but my body made a kind of kink—or maybe you could say I kind of wiggled. Anyway, I managed to change my approach just enough to go through without touching the Needle, and I made the fall without any trouble.

I don't think anyone could have noticed the slight amount I was off, and the crowd really did clap. In fact, it was a standing ovation. It made me really glad for the Cortina Brothers' Circus!

Then, I ran back to do the Slingshot finale, but I could see something was terribly wrong! I stopped dead still, because it looked like a fight.

Joe was lying on the ground trying to get up, Felipe was held in a hammerlock by his brother Thomas, and Angel was crying and pulling at his arms!

"What is it?" I shouted as I ran up. "What's going on?"

I was glad that we were really in the dark, outside the ring of light that flooded the center ring. Angel turned a tearful face toward me and said, "Felipe! *He's* the Phantom, Barney!"

I stood there staring at them. Then Mr. Cortina said, "I saw him, Barney, my own brother! He reached out and changed the dial of the tension gauge just before Joe pulled the trigger! You could have been killed!"

He released Felipe just enough to turn him around and look into his face. Felipe seemed wild, not at all like the nice, sweet guy I'd been rooming with. His eyes were rolling around in his head, and he was almost frothing at the mouth. When he tried to say something, he screamed like a madman!

"You always got *everything!*" he shouted at his brother. "You got Lillian, and you had a family! You stole the circus from me, Thomas! You stole it!"

"I always gave you anything you asked for," Mr. Cortina said gently.

"*Gave* me! You gave me?" Felipe shouted, trying to break loose from his brother's grip. "You cheated me! My own brother, and you cheated me! I could have been the greatest flier in the world, but you dropped me! And you did it on purpose so you could have Lillian! You did it on purpose!"

Lillian Cortina was standing there, sorrow all over her face. Then she said quietly, "Thomas, you must go up to catch Barney." Then she took Felipe by the arm, and he grew quiet at once. "Come, Felipe, we must go talk about all this, all right?"

Felipe stopped struggling and looked at her with a dreamy look in his large brown eyes. "All right, Lillian. Yes, we will talk. I must tell you about what we will do!"

She led him away as the ringmaster was introducing the final performance of the Super Circus—the Slingshot Catch. We watched her lead Felipe like a child into the darkness to the dressing room, and Mr. Cortina muttered, "I never knew he felt like that!"

"Thomas," Lou said sharply, "get up in the traps! You have to catch Barney! Can you do it?"

Thomas Cortina had been a performer all his life. He shrugged his muscular shoulders. "Yes, I can do it. Barney, do not be afraid. I will catch you if I have to climb down to the sawdust to do it!"

He disappeared, and Lou said, "Barney, get ready!"

I climbed into the sled, my mind humming like crazy. Lou stood beside me whispering, "Barney, this time forget about yourself! I know you've been holding back. You've never stopped thinking about yourself—about what might happen if Thomas didn't catch you. I understand! But now, it's time for you to say, 'If I fall, I fall!' Trust in the hands of your catcher!"

"I . . . don't think I can!" I gasped.

He shook me with his iron hand. "You're a Christian, you tell me. Well, sooner or later you'll have to trust God! Isn't that right? You'll have to turn loose of everything and say, 'Well, God, if you let me fall, it's all over!'"

"I . . . I guess so!"

"Well, this one time, Barney Buck, put your trust in Thomas Cortina! Just let him do the worrying, and you trust those strong hands of his! Will you do it, Barney?"

The drums were beginning to roll, and I couldn't think too clearly. Then I made up my mind that, for once in my life, I'd just do one thing for somebody *else,* instead of for Barney! My eyes were wide open when I prayed a little prayer: "Lord, please give Thomas whatever he needs, because I'm going for broke this time!"

Sometimes I thought I was too free and easy with God, shooting off prayers like that. But Coach had told me once that Jonah had done the same thing in the belly of a whale. So, I guessed it was OK!

It was time to show my stuff. I looked up. There was Mr. Cortina way up at the very top of the Garden. He looked like a doll way up there, swinging back and forth. My chances of flying through the air and getting to him at the exact split second when our hands would join didn't seem possible!

Then Lou said, "You ready, Barney?"

"Anytime!" I whispered.

I felt the Slingshot tremble, and there was the familiar *whirrrr-thump*. Suddenly I was on my way to those hands!

Nothing but a flash of color, and my eyes were fixed on Mr. Cortina. I rose up like a bird, keeping my body straight and my eyes wide open. It was a little like going off Joe's ol' catapult into the Caddo River, but this time thousands of people were watching!

Mr. Cortina was on his backswing. He moved forward. My hands were out, and this time I didn't even think about the net. I just kept my hands out.

Mr. Cortina zoomed in, growing larger as he came closer. Suddenly his strong hands were in front of me. I resisted the sudden temptation to double up and fall to the net. I kept my body straight and knew if he missed me . . . I didn't even have time to think about that!

He didn't miss.

There was a slapping sound as his hands clamped down on my forearms like a vise. I grabbed his arms, but even if I hadn't, I couldn't fall.

The cymbals clashed, and a roar of applause rocked the air. I hung there as Mr. Cortina held me, and we swung back and forth as the crowd went crazy.

Finally he lifted me up, and I managed to sit beside him on the swing and give a wave to the sea of faces below.

By now everybody was standing and yelling. Mr. Cortina said, while he held me tightly on the bar, "You have saved my circus, Barney. Thank you!"

That was worth it all! Somehow we got down. I still don't remember how. Then all the performers were standing before the judges' stand for the awards ceremony. The Cortina Brothers' Circus won their share. Rex Rogers won the Animal Act Award, and of course, Lou Beauchamp won the Clown Award.

But finally they got to the big one—the New Act Award.

I was standing next to Mr. Cortina when I heard the announcement: "And for the Best New Act of the Year, the prize goes to Barney Buck of the Cortina Brothers' Circus!"

The place went plumb wild! People were yelling and screaming, and then Angel and Dee Dee came up and hugged me and kissed me. What a drag!

The biggest thrill was seeing Debra and Uncle Dave, who'd driven up secretly to surprise me. Debra hugged me, too, but she said, "You just wait till you get back to Goober Holler, Barney Buck! I'll show you!"

Finally Joe and Jake and I began to say good-bye to everyone.

Lou Beauchamp gave us bear hugs and told us he'd miss all three of us.

Juan was pretty good! He said to me in a whisper,

"You're a real kinker, Barney! Angel and me, we won't forget you!"

I had an idea that Angel would finally wind up in a double act with Juan. The thought even came to me that she'd used me just to make him jealous. I always said you had to be careful with those acrobats!

Rex Rogers and Dee Dee came around to say good-bye. Ruth was hanging onto Rex's arm, and I saw by the light in Dee Dee's face that she wouldn't be lonesome very long!

Eventually we said good-bye to all of the circus people, and it wasn't easy. We'd found out that they weren't different from the people at Goober Holler! People are pretty much the same no matter where you find them.

Mr. Cortina gripped my hand. "Barney, if you ever want to come back, there is a place for you, you hear?" he said, wiping something from his eye.

"Mr. Cortina, what'll happen to Felipe? I mean, will he go to jail or something?"

A sad look crossed his face. "No, not that. Maybe to a counselor. We will see. I blame myself for much of Felipe's trouble." He shook his head. "I should have been quicker to see what was happening."

"Well, I'll write him when I get home. He was real ~d to me, and I still think a lot of him."

~. Cortina grinned and gave me a hug. "You are a

real trouper, Barney Buck! You have made a real believer out of me—about this thing called prayer. The Cortinas will not forget. One more thing, Barney. Please call me Thomas. I want you to think of me as your friend."

"Oh, sure, Thomas!" I said with a wide grin. Somehow, it hadn't bothered me to call him Mr. Cortina, but I appreciated him saying that anyway.

Then Jake and Joe and I went back to our motel room, and Uncle Dave and Debra helped us pack. Of course, Debra helped out mostly with Joe's stuff. I wouldn't let any girl get her hands on my things!

Finally we were ready. "How 'bout gettin' a bite to eat?" Uncle Dave suggested. That sounded good to us, so we headed for the nearest McDonald's, which in New York wasn't the easiest place to find, with the traffic and all.

It took us three days to drive back to Cedarville, but we enjoyed ourselves on the way. It was a lot more fun than when we'd left Chicago for Cedarville, I could say that much! Anyway, we got back to our home place in Goober Holler, and things seemed pretty dull. Compared to our circus days, what wouldn't?

Debra must've noticed my moping around, because she organized a swimming party on the Ouachita River. That would probably be the last one of the season since it was getting cold.

To tell the truth, I almost didn't go. It seemed too tame after the center ring at Madison Square Garden. I just shrugged when Debra asked me to go. "I don't much think I'll come, Debra. It's too cold."

She gave me a look out of those dark eyes of hers and put her hands on her hips. "Too tame for you, is it, Showboat?"

That made me blush. Ever since I'd gotten back to Goober Holler, she'd called me that when she thought I was getting a little bit too big for Cedarville.

"Gee, you don't have to call me that all the time," I said, and I knew I'd better go.

We all met at the Tree, an old cypress with limbs sticking out at all angles. It was at a good wide place in the river where we could swim and mess around. Everyone was there—all the kids I ran around with at school. We had a bunch of food—marshmallows, hot dogs, soda, Twinkies, and other junk food guaranteed to ruin your digestive system. It was fun yelling and swimming and having a great time. All of a sudden I realized it was good to be home again. The circus had been exciting, but it wasn't like *home,* you know?

Just when things seemed to be winding down at the party, Debra got the idea to show off by jumping off a limb of the Tree!

The Tree was a sort of symbol for us kids. If you could go diving off the first limb into the river, you were a "one-limmer." If you had the nerve to climb up to the next limb and dive off, you were a "two-limmer."

Not to brag or anything, but I was a *five*-limmer. That was the best there was. Fred Dickens was a four-limmer, but up until then I was the only five-limmer in the crowd.

The gang all gave a cheer of delight when Debra climbed up that tree and did a beautiful swan dive right off the fifth limb.

Of course, Jake had to say, "She can't do that to you, Barney! Get up there and show that ol' girl not to fool around with us Bucks!"

As I've said before, Jake was pretty free when it came to risking my body! But this time I didn't need to be nudged. I glared at Debra standing waist-deep in the river, grinning at me, just daring me to do any better!

While I was sweating it out in the circus, Debra had been working all summer long at going off that fifth limb! Just to spite me, I bet.

I got up and walked with a swagger over to the Tree and started climbing it. I didn't even slow down at the fifth limb, but just kept right on climbing. When I went past the seventh limb and felt the slender top of the cypress sway, there was a sudden silence down below.

Then Debra shouted, "Barney, don't be silly! You'll get hurt!"

Let her beg! I thought as I scrambled to the top and hung on like a monkey.

17

Then I wished I hadn't! I was swaying the way Maureen Walsh had in the center ring when her husband, Fritz, had held her on top of a stainless-steel pole! She'd done all kinds of stunts way up there, but all I wanted to do was hold on!

Then Debra called for me to come down again, and I let go with one hand and hollered, "Look out below! Here comes Barney Buck! The Pride of Goober Holler doing his death-defying plunge. Ta-daaaaa!"

The cypress was swaying so bad I was just as likely to land on the ground as in the river, but I wasn't going to let Debra show me up! So, I waited until the slender top swayed out over the river before letting go!

Then just about everything that *could* go wrong, went wrong! In the first place, I didn't do a graceful dive like Debra. Mine resembled a wild possum waving its arms and legs like crazy!

I didn't get far enough out over the water, so even though I'd managed to twist in the air enough to go into the river headfirst, the water wasn't very deep. I tried to make that little twist, flipping up to stay away from the bottom, but I didn't make it!

I was pretty lucky even hitting the river, but I was driven straight to the bottom, which was nothing but soft black mud. I went down so hard I went up to my neck in that yukky stuff!

I had enough air so I didn't drown, but when I came

up, my eyes were packed with mud. I couldn't see any more than a worm! My ears were stuffed with mud and so was my mouth.

I felt blind, deaf, and dumb! Jake told me later I'd lost my sense of direction and started downstream, instead of making for the bank. I would have drowned if someone hadn't pulled me out.

Guess who that *someone* was! Debra Simmons.

She grabbed me by my muddy hair and dragged me back to the bank, where I stood sputtering and spitting mud.

By then everybody saw I was all right, and they were all doubled over, laughing as if something funny had happened. They were saying things like "Hey, Showboat, you better clean up your act!" and other dumb stuff they thought was funny.

I was trying to figure out a way to sneak home to Tim, but Debra kept on dabbing at me with a towel until I was pretty well cleaned up. I must've looked sad, because she gave my face a little pat and said, "Don't pay any attention to them, Barney. *I* still think you're wonderful!"

Well, that wasn't too bad, you know? I gave a little grin and wiped at some of the mud that still clung to me. "What about this mess?"

Without answering, Debra gave me a kiss on my cheek in front of the whole crowd. She laughed, then hollered out loud, "Why, Barney, *that's show biz!*"

If you've enjoyed **The Ozark Adventures,**
you'll want to read these additional series!

Forbidden Doors *(New! Fall 1994)*
As Rebecca and Scott discover the danger of the occult,
they learn to put their trust in God.

#1 The Society   0-8423-5922-2

#2 The Deceived   0-8423-1352-4

The Last Chance Detectives *(New! Fall 1994)*
Four young sleuths tackle local mysteries from their restored
B-17 bomber—and develop faith in God's guidance. Also on video!

#1 Mystery Lights of Navajo Mesa   0-8423-2082-2

Choice Adventures
These books let you create the story by choosing your own plot!
Join the Ringers in sixteen adventures, including these latest releases:

#13 Mountain Bike Mayhem   0-8423-5131-0

#14 The Mayan Mystery   0-8423-5132-9

#15 The Appalachian Ambush   0-8423-5133-7

#16 The Overnight Ordeal   0-8423-5134-5

McGee and Me!
Meet Nick Martin, a normal kid with an unusual friend: the lively,
animated McGee! All titles also available on video.

#1 The Big Lie   0-8423-4169-2

#2 A Star in the Breaking   0-8423-4168-4

#3 The Not-So-Great Escape   0-8423-4167-6

#4 Skate Expectations   0-8423-4165-X

#5 Twister and Shout   0-8423-4166-8

#6 Back to the Drawing Board   0-8423-4111-0

#7 Do the Bright Thing   0-8423-4112-9

#8 Take Me Out of the Ball Game   0-8423-4113-7

#9 'Twas the Fight Before Christmas   0-8423-4114-5

#10 In the Nick of Time   0-8423-4122-6

#11 The Blunder Years   0-8423-4123-4

#12 Beauty in the Least   0-8423-4124-2